"Are you okay?"

"I'm great." Logan shifted so Kat wouldn't see the bullet tear just above his shoulder blade. The wound wasn't bad, and he welcomed the pain. Better the one in his body than the one ripping through his heart.

"Logan—" she began.

"Don't, Kat. Not yet." He didn't know what to feel except that he had two kids out there who could be in danger and their mother had lied to him for three years. She could have found him any time she wanted. Lived like the princess she apparently was in real life.

The SUV pulled up to a small, wood-sided house.

Kat clutched at the door handle but Logan gripped the latch to keep her from opening it.

Kat glared at Logan. "I'm going in. They're *my* kids."

His temper blew. "Get this straight, princess. Those are my kids, too, and we're going to have one hell of a talk about *that* once everyone's out and safe."

ROBIN PERINI

CHRISTMAS CONSPIRACY

HARLEQUIN®
entertain, enrich, inspire™

For the real Lanie and Hayden—and their amazing big sister, Haley.
You are the light of my heart, dear ones. I love you. Always and Forever.

Sometimes a book takes sheer grit and will to finish. I'm blessed to have
a best friend who stood beside me. This one is yours, Claire.
Because you not only had my back, you carried me!

ISBN-13: 978-0-373-69648-2

CHRISTMAS CONSPIRACY

Copyright © 2012 by Robin L. Perini

Recycling programs
for this product may
not exist in your area.

www.Harlequin.com

Printed in U.S.A.

ABOUT THE AUTHOR

Award-winning author Robin Perini's love of heart-stopping suspense and poignant romance, coupled with her adoration of high-tech weaponry and covert ops, encouraged her secret inner commando to take on the challenge of writing romantic suspense novels. Her mission's motto: "When danger and romance collide, no heart is safe."

Devoted to giving her readers fast-paced, high-stakes adventures with a love story sure to melt their hearts, Robin won the prestigious Romance Writers of America Golden Heart Award in 2011. By day she works for an advanced technology corporation, and in her spare time you might find her giving one of her many nationally acclaimed writing workshops or training in competitive small-bore rifle silhouette shooting. Robin loves to interact with readers. You can catch her on her website, www.robinperini.com, several major social-networking sites or write to her at P.O. Box 50472, Albuquerque, NM 87181-0472.

Books by Robin Perini

HARLEQUIN INTRIGUE
1340—FINDING HER SON
1362—COWBOY IN THE CROSSFIRE
1381—CHRISTMAS CONSPIRACY

All backlist available in ebook. Don't miss any of our special offers. Write to us at the following address for information on our newest releases.

Harlequin Reader Service
U.S.: 3010 Walden Ave., P.O. Box 1325, Buffalo, NY 14269

Canadian: P.O. Box 609, Fort Erie, Ont. L2A 5X3

CAST OF CHARACTERS

Katherine "Kat" Nelson—Can this unexpected heir to the throne and Texas-born mother of twins protect her children from an international conspiracy by relying on the man who betrayed her—her children's father?

Logan Carmichael—His clandestine past has made him the best private investigator money can buy. Now he'll need every skill he possesses to keep the woman who broke his heart and their children alive.

Hayden and Lanie—Katherine's children don't know the meaning of fear and have no idea their very existence is a threat to a man willing to do anything for money and power.

Prince Stefan of Bellevaux—The heir to the throne lived on the edge and was horrified to discover the identity of the traitor to his country before an explosion in the throne room silenced him. Will the truth ever be uncovered?

Roland, Duke of Sarbonne—His ancestor ruled Bellevaux, but Roland needs more than history to solidify his position in the king's eyes. Perhaps marriage to a princess?

Daniel Adams—Framed for the assassination of Prince Stefan, then imprisoned and tortured for his knowledge, can Daniel warn Logan of the true threat before it's too late?

King Leopold of Bellevaux—He has lost two sons to assassination. Now he has found a daughter and heiress. How far will he go to save his kingdom?

Prologue

"We start again," the voice echoed down the hall, sliding through the bars to reach Daniel.

He hated the perfect English accent, could feel himself sweat awaiting his own daily interrogation.

"Why did King Leopold hire Logan Carmichael again?"

A gut-wrenching howl echoed through the prison's stone passageway. Daniel flinched. If only he could manage to escape, but beaten and bound to a chair, he was at the sadist's mercy.

"Traitor," the unknown prisoner down the hall challenged.

"Silence! I have more than one way of getting this information, and you are not that important to me. The so-called security expert should be disgraced for not preventing the massacre in the throne room, not trusted with more assignments." A whip cracked across flesh. "What has Carmichael been commanded to do?"

Daniel tried to force his eyes open, but they'd swollen shut, and dried blood sealed the lids tight. He yanked on his ropes. A warm trail of liquid coursed over his hands and fingers. Maybe he just imagined the sensation. He'd lost feeling in his arms hours ago and his shoulders had gone numb.

The sharp lash of a whip sounded again and again.

"Why is Carmichael in Texas? Answer me."

The beating didn't stop.

If Logan was really in Texas, Daniel was doomed. No one else knew he'd been in Bellevaux. No one except his boss's enemy. A sour burning scorched Daniel's throat.

The man screamed.

"Carmichael is not at his ranch in Carder. Where is he?"

Daniel jolted. His torturers knew too much. Daniel knew too much. God, he wished he could forget. He'd been a fool. He should've told Logan his suspicions from the beginning. Logan wouldn't know the betrayer was so close. Daniel couldn't break or he would betray Logan, too.

An ominous silence fell, and foreboding gripped Daniel's chest like a fist. He couldn't breathe as he waited. No sound came from the room.

Crack!

A teeth-clenched groan.

"Not ready to talk? You have one hundred twenty-six bones in all. Do you have a preference?"

Crack!

An unholy scream.

Daniel shuddered.

Finally, one word.

"Princess." The man moaned. "Heir to throne."

A sharp curse exploded with the whip's next slash. A loud crash splintered through the prison. "Revive him! I want to know who the princess is and where she is."

"No," Daniel whispered. "Don't tell." He had to get word to Logan. But how?

With a clang, the metal door down the hall banged open. Sweat slipped from Daniel's brow, and his gut tensed, the response instinctive now. Heavy boots pounded toward his cell, then slowed and paused at his cell. Daniel clamped his swollen eyes tighter, using pain to sharpen his senses. He would fight them. They wouldn't get what they wanted. He'd die first.

He prayed he'd die first.

Murmurs filtered from outside the cell. "Open it, and let me know when the other one is conscious. Although…I may be here for a while."

With his vision impaired, at least Daniel didn't have to look at the satisfied expression on his interrogator's face. He hated the guy's icy smile. Hated that the man and his cohorts had killed so many people and no one suspected.

More than that, because of their torture, the bastards knew more than Logan did and had planned accordingly. Without intel, even a legendary former CIA operative like Logan Carmichael could be ambushed. Daniel's capture was proof of that.

"So, the silence has been broken," his tormentor taunted.

The squeaking iron door made Daniel's stomach lurch. His thighs clenched, his shoulders hunched. He wanted to shrink into nothing, but fought his weakness. Even so, each soft sound of the whip slapping against his captor's hand stung like a burning welt against Daniel's skin.

"I've discovered you work for Logan Carmichael. You shouldn't keep such secrets from me, but I guarantee you won't keep many more."

Heavy metal clanged on the iron table beside Daniel's chair.

Oh, God.

The interrogator trailed the leather grip of the whip

across Daniel's cheek. "Give me what I want, my friend, and maybe you'll live. Right now, *you* are the suspected terrorist who bombed the Bellevaux throne room and killed Prince Stefan. I produce your body and I'm a hero. No one will question what shape you're in when found dead. You're assumed dead now."

The man leaned closer. "Only *I* can clear your name. Now, where is Carmichael going and who is this princess?"

"Go to hell." Daniel braced himself. The whip came crashing across his face and the force of the blow sent the chair toppling. Daniel's head slammed into the floor. *Logan, be on guard. Protect her.*

"Prepare him!"

The guards grabbed Daniel's shoulders. Knife blades of pain shot through his arms as they cut the ropes binding him to the chair. They rammed him against the stone wall, face-first, then tethered his wrists to metal rings high on the wall. Daniel arched in agony as the whip slashed his already raw back.

"Where is Carmichael and who is the girl?" The man's voice was deadly cold.

"I don't know."

"Bring the wrench."

Daniel went cold inside, then laughed bitterly. At least if the guy stuck to this line of questioning, Daniel wouldn't betray Logan. Daniel *didn't* know where his boss was or who the princess could possibly be. The first blow of the wrench smashed his left hand. His tortured scream filled his mind and body like an air-raid siren set at the highest decibel, but no sound ever escaped his clenched lips.

Please, God, let me die fast.

Chapter One

Logan Carmichael catapulted into the fiery barn, sparks and large embers singeing his leather bomber jacket and burning through his jeans. He could barely see through the black smoke billowing from his right, but its heat scorched his lungs. Desperation clawed his insides as he raced toward the woman who had broken his heart three years ago. Now that he'd finally found her, he wouldn't lose her again. Not this way.

"Kat!" He grabbed her bare arm. "What are you doing? The barn won't last much longer."

She spun around, her eyes frantic at first, then widening in shocked recognition. "We've got to save the horses," she yelled over the roar of the fire and the shrill sounds of the frantic animals.

"I'm getting you out of here."

"We can still rescue them." She tugged against his hold. "Take your shirt off and cover their eyes. If they can't see the fire, you can lead them out safely. Please, Logan."

The inferno exploded through the roof on the far side. More sparks rained down. It wouldn't take long to engulf the entire building.

Barely visible through the thickening haze, two horses whinnied in fear. Logan cursed. They were running out of time. "I'll do whatever you say if it gets you out of here."

Kat twisted away and dove into the first stall. She stripped down to her tank top, then tied her plaid flannel shirt around the filly's head. Offering words of encouragement between hacking coughs, Kat backed out of the stall, hauling the terrified mare with her.

Logan took the reins and shoved Kat toward the barn door. Heat seared his hands and face the closer he got to the fire. He fought with the huge animal every step. "Call for help. I'll get them both out."

For the first time since he'd met Kat three years ago, she didn't argue. He stripped off his jacket and shirt, then went back for the second horse, while she ran to the open door. When he glanced up, he could barely make out the blue winter skies through the smoke-filled opening. The fire was moving fast.

Just before she reached the barn door, it slammed shut.

She skidded to a halt, then tugged at the door. It didn't budge. "It's locked!" Kat shouted over the roar of flames. "We're trapped!"

She pounded on the wood, screaming for help, then dissolved into fits of coughing as the toxic smoke swirled thicker.

Logan knew no one would come. This fire was no accident. That was clear the moment the door closed. Someone wanted them to burn.

"Cover your mouth with your bandana and come with me," he shouted across the large room. He used his black T-shirt to filter the sooty air and squinted through the roiling flames that licked the back and side of the wooden structure. They couldn't risk going out the front now, anyway. No telling who waited.

Logan cursed King Leopold as he threw his jacket on and pulled the two horses to the intact side of the barn. He tied them off. The conniving ruler had obviously kept more than a few secrets from Logan when he hired him to find Kat for the second time. This one might cost them their lives.

The blindfolded horses reared, then stomped down, panic-stricken, but Logan couldn't calm the animals now. Kat would have to take care of them. Fortunately, she had a mesmerizing effect on animals, because the two were crazed right now. The fire had engulfed the front of the barn in the past few minutes. He didn't have long to break through the side of the structure and get Kat and the horses out before the place collapsed or became one giant inferno.

He grabbed a sledgehammer from a stack of tools in the corner and swung the heavy mallet against the siding. Wooden boards shattered and a small hole yielded daylight. Fresh air streamed into the foggy barn. Again and again, he cracked the old beams, then kicked them free until the resulting gap was big enough for Kat and the horses to pass through. The large cool rush of air fed the fire. Flames licked closer and hotter. The horses screamed in fear as burning rafters and boards toppled and crashed closer and closer.

"Kat, the barn is going! We have to leave now!"

Coughing violently, Kat grabbed the two horses and dragged them toward the opening. At the last minute, she yanked off their blindfolds and the animals bolted through the ragged gap to freedom.

Logan had just reached for her when, with an ominous creaking sound, the metal roof directly above Kat's head gave way and a heavy sheet fell.

"Watch out!" Logan dropped the sledgehammer and leaped at her.

Kat ducked, but the metal slammed her head and knocked her to the ground. Logan lifted the hot corrugated sheet and shoved it aside.

She lay still. Far too still.

Logan scooped her into his arms and held her close against his chest as he carried her to the opening that he could barely see through his blurred vision. He tried to convince himself that his eyes only watered from the heat and smoke, and not from the sheer terror he felt at the limp form of the woman cradled in his arms.

She couldn't be dead, but she would be if they didn't escape. The fire was nearly on them now. He yanked his Glock free and almost rushed outside, but an odd sound made him hesitate at the last instant. Was that an engine? Was the person who trapped them leaving, thinking they were dead? Or had the killer seen the horses escape and moved closer?

Another rafter fell, just missing Logan and Kat, and setting the area next to them on fire. No choice. They had to leave or die. He hauled Kat over his shoulder, then palmed the gun and edged through the opening.

He didn't see anyone, but every instinct screamed imminent danger. A grove of oak stood a few hundred yards away. They'd provide cover. If he could get her there.

Just as he rushed out of the barn with her in his arms, a bullet thwacked into the wood over his head.

Hell.

Around the corner of the barn, a man in a black mask took aim from the window of a beat-up red truck. Mud covered the plate.

Logan turned sideways to shield Kat and fired in one fluid motion. The bullet ripped into the man's shoulder.

He swore and his gun dropped to the ground outside the truck.

Logan quickly set Kat down away from the barn and headed for the vehicle, his gun in hand. "Get out of the truck!" Logan yelled over the roar of the blaze behind him. "Face in the dirt. Now!"

The masked man's eyes squinted at the Bowie glinting on the dashboard, then at the gun lying in the dirt. Logan could see the cogs rolling in the shooter's mind, gauging the layout between them. Logan's finger tensed against the trigger, but they both knew it wasn't a clean shot.

With a quick move, the guy dove away from the window, out of Logan's line of sight, and slammed the truck in gear. Within seconds, Texas dust kicked up as the tires spun out.

Logan took a few more shots, but the truck had gone too far for the handgun to be accurate. Heat seared Logan's back. He glanced behind him at the burning barn, redirecting the remaining adrenaline from his anger, and carried Kat to the stand of oak trees.

He sank in the grass and dirt and knelt next to her. Her head lolled to the side. The light hit her face. Her lips were tinged blue. Despite the heat pouring at them from the burning barn, everything inside him froze. "No."

In seconds, he'd slanted her head back and forced breath into her lungs. Once. Twice.

She remained still.

He clasped her face in his hands. "Don't do this, Kat! Stay with me."

The fire and shooter had almost got them. He wouldn't lose her now. He slammed two more breaths into her, willing them to be enough, then clutched her to him, rocking her against his body. "Come on. Breathe, dammit."

Suddenly, she sucked in a deep breath, shuddered and started coughing.

"Kat?" He cupped her cheek, his touch tender, his hand trembling.

Her eyes fluttered. "Look after them," she whispered. "Promise...."

"The horses are out, Kat. You saved them. You're going to be fine."

She opened her lips as if to say more, then groaned and her head fell back.

He sent up a prayer and felt for her pulse. The regular thud restarted his heart.

She was breathing more regularly, but beneath the soot, her face had gone pale as cream. He gently touched the goose egg on her head, and his gut twisted. She could've been killed. How had this happened? Logan looked around the deserted Daughtery ranch where she worked. Why hadn't anyone shown up for a burning barn?

Well, one thing was for sure. He and Kat couldn't stay here in case their attacker had friends to finish what he'd started.

"Kat, honey, wake up."

Logan willed her to regain consciousness. Her chest rose and fell, but those icy baby blues remained closed. She'd been out too long. He needed help.

He sent a code through his unit's pagers to have the doc and a full security team meet him at the rendezvous hotel. He wished he could take her to a hospital, but he couldn't risk the exposure. If she didn't wake up soon, though, he'd have no choice.

Quickly, he swept the car for bombs, grabbed the attacker's gun for evidence, then lifted Kat high in his arms. Her softness settled against him. Memories of holding her assailed his mind. He hugged her close before carefully placing her in the truck.

As he pulled out of the ranch, Logan tugged his cell phone from his pocket and tapped out a number.

"Yes," a harsh growl answered through the earpiece.

"Sergei, get His *Majesty* on the phone," Logan said, his own voice raspy, but his tone brooking no argument from the flunky on the other end of the call. "Now!"

A few whispers sounded in the background.

"You dare command me, *Mr.* Carmichael?"

Logan could imagine the tic near King Leopold's eye. The man's obvious tell showed his anger, but he had nothing on Logan's current fury. He should've known the ruler of Bellevaux was up to something when King Leopold ordered Katherine Nelson brought to him. The assignment didn't make any more sense now than when he'd instructed Logan to find her three years ago, then the king had abruptly ordered Logan to drop the investigation after he'd sent in the preliminary report.

"You better start talking, Your Majesty. You lied to me. There's nothing simple about this job, and Katherine Nelson isn't coming near you without an explanation."

"Your contract is with me. I sign your paycheck. Therefore, your loyalty is mine."

"You're not getting this. An innocent woman was nearly burned alive this morning and then shot at. You held out on me."

"Someone tried to kill her?" The king gasped. "Nothing can happen to her, Carmichael. If she dies, all is lost."

"She's not going to die," Logan snapped. "But if I'm to protect her, you have to let me in on your big secret.

What's your interest in her? Why does someone want her dead?"

The king let out a frustrated sigh. "What I'm about to tell ~~you goes no further~~ than us. No one in your company or your government must learn of this. Do I have your guarantee?"

Logan tamped down his urge to reach through the phone and choke Leopold. Logan's international security firm had handled dozens of highly sensitive issues for the family in the five years since he'd left the CIA. "You've never doubted my word before."

"You promised to protect my dead son," the king said flatly. "His assassination is on your head."

Logan stilled at the truth.

Prince Stefan had died in the throne room bombing. The M.O. had matched Logan's top operative and good friend, Daniel Adams. Rumors of terrorists' payoffs and betrayal still raced through the intelligence community.

For Logan, it was personal. Prince Stefan had been more than an assignment. He'd been Logan's friend, too. He didn't know what to believe. Logan found Daniel's complicity impossible to grasp, but the mounting evidence had been hard to ignore.

If the accusations were true, Logan *was* ultimately responsible. He'd personally sent Daniel to Bellevaux, undercover, to infiltrate the king's ranks and find the ruler's enemies.

"You have my word I'll keep Kat safe," Logan said, softly. "Your trust in me is not misplaced."

"Very well." The king took a deep breath. "With Stefan dead, I need to designate an heir by Christmas. If I do not choose someone with a royal bloodline, my country loses its sovereignty and will be divided between Germany and France."

Awareness of what the king was about to say hit Logan like a fist to the gut. His dream of a second chance with Kat destroyed before he acknowledged wanting it. "You don't mean that Kat is—"

"Katherine Nelson is my daughter," the ruler of Bellevaux said. "She is the sole surviving heir to the throne."

Logan's hand reached over and caressed Kat's smooth cheek. She was still beautiful, but now out of reach. He had only one job. Protect her. With two attempts on her life in the last half hour, Kat might be the sole heir, but someone didn't intend for her to survive for long.

THE PILLOWS WERE SOFT, the blanket plush and thick—nothing like the cheap, scratchy wool throw on her bed at home. Kat ran her fingers over the mink-soft cover. She didn't want to open her eyes. She'd been having the weirdest dream. She had to wake up, though. Something was wrong. She just couldn't remember what. She groaned, hating the headache that made her dread opening her eyes. Everything within her rejected the idea of letting in the light.

Her head throbbed, and her throat was raw. She raised her hand to her forehead, then slid her fingers over and pressed them against the bandage covering her left temple. She winced as she probed the injury. She tried to move her other hand, but something weighed it down.

Kat forced her eyes open, blinking painfully as light speared into her skull. A quick glance revealed an IV pole hanging beside her, hooked to her arm. Panic hit. Was she in a hospital? She couldn't afford one. How long had she been out? Where were her children?

She struggled to a seated position and tried to make sense of the room spinning around her. This looked more like a hotel than a hospital.

What was going on?

She couldn't think clearly. Something important. She had to remember. Her thoughts scattered. She felt drugged. Whatever medication was in that IV had to go. She pulled at the bandages until she freed herself from the tube and the needle.

A voice filtered in from the next room.

"Rafe, I want you and Hunter on this one. I need people who know the players and the stakes."

It couldn't be. The voice from three years ago. A voice that made her shiver with longing—and hurt. She'd thought never again to see the man who'd nearly stolen her heart. Logan Carmichael.

His velvet tones had whispered in her ear in the dark. She'd shuddered under his touch, then she'd run, overwhelmed by what she'd felt for him. When she'd finally tried to reach him, she'd been turned away. Life, she'd learned all too well, gave no second chances.

"You still have surveillance on the king and his entourage?" Logan listened, then let out a low curse. "The fool. I'll be ready."

Logan's voice was so cold, so deadly. Kat shook her head to clear it, then groaned. Why was she here in a hotel? She'd been at her weekend job. She'd been dreaming about Logan. Crazy dreams. Dangerous dreams about horses…and fire.

Memories flashed. The fire! She gasped for air. "Logan!"

She struggled to her feet and the room swirled around her.

Someone had locked them in the barn.

Someone had tried to kill them.

Logan dashed into the room, catching her as she fell

against the nearby bureau. "What are you doing out of bed?"

She clung to him, hating the way the room spun in crazy circles. "I don't know what we're doing here, but I have to leave. Now. Oh, God, how long have I been out?"

"A couple hours. You've been sedated."

"I have to go home." *The twins.* They'd be upset. It had to be at least noon. And Paulina, the babysitter. Kat was so late. She tried to push past Logan. "I have responsibilities."

Logan placed her back on the bed, and pressed her shoulders into the down pillow. He hovered over her. "You were severely dehydrated, suffering from exhaustion, thrashing and crying out in your sleep. I couldn't take a chance that you'd hurt yourself."

She stared into his face, struggling to keep it in focus, stunned he wasn't a dream. She'd had enough over the past three years to wonder. She blinked. He was real. He'd changed. Oh, his brown hair was still cut short, a tad longer than a military cut, and he'd lost some weight, but more than that. His hazel eyes were stressed and tired in his lean face, but she also saw something in them she didn't expect. Concern? Worry? For her?

Feeling woozy, unable to help herself, she let her hand hover over the scar marring his cheek, a scar that hadn't been there three years ago. She wanted to touch him, but she couldn't let herself. She had more than her own wishes to think about now. "I need to go home. You have to take me there."

He clasped her hand in his. "Kat, it's going to have to wait."

"Not happening, Logan. I need to leave and there's something I have to tell you on the way. You're not going to li—"

The bedroom door slammed open.

"What do you think you're doing, Carmichael? You will not touch her."

A distinguished man, his salt-and-pepper hair perfectly styled, and dressed in a suit that must have cost two years' salary, strode in. He acted as if he owned the world, and two hulking figures trailed behind him like mindless minions.

Logan turned, shielding her from view. Kat shoved at him to move aside but he planted his feet and crossed his arms over his chest.

"Are you *trying* to get her killed?" Logan's soft voice dripped ice from every word. "I told you not to come here. What if you were followed?"

One of the burly bodyguards pushed to the fore. "You will not speak to His Majesty in that tone."

Without moving, Logan stared the man down. "Back off, Sergei. I'm in no mood to play protocol games. I said I'd arrange the meet."

"And no one commands the King of Bellevaux," the ruler snapped, his accent deepening. "My business cannot wait. I have less than two weeks to ensure my daughter doesn't embarrass me or her country."

Kat leaned against the bed, the king's words swirling in her mind. Okay, the sedative might still be wreaking havoc in her system, but the royal invasion had been doing a fine job of clearing her head until that bizarre comment. Who was this guy's daughter?

Logan's voice turned lower and deadlier. "And I'm responsible for making sure Kat stays alive, which you don't seem to care about since you kept her true identity from me until it was almost too late."

The king's face reddened. "You found her. I'm here to claim her. Now step away from my daughter!"

"Excuse me? I'm *not* an object, and I am definitely *not* your daughter." Kat peered around Logan and tumbled over the side of the bed, landing in a heap. He knelt to help her, but she shoved him aside and stood, fighting the dizziness. "Logan, what's going on? Who is this joker?" she asked, praying her head would stop pounding.

Her ex-lover turned, and she gasped at the tension in his jaw making his scar stand out in relief. Logan let out a stream of air. "He's your father. King Leopold of Bellevaux. You are Princess Katherine, his only heir."

No. This couldn't be happening.

"*That's* why you showed up out of nowhere this morning? For *him?*"

The truth flickered in Logan's guilty gaze.

A fledgling hope that he'd come for her after all this time went up in flames as hot and deadly as the barn fire. More and more of the sedative's effect faded. She turned away from Logan to stare at the stranger who was supposedly her father. *King* Leopold. Impossible. She felt no bond with him.

The man, wearing Armani, looked her up and down as if he were studying a filly to purchase. "Good cheekbones. Passable figure. Maybe we can gloss over the cowgirl foolishness. I think we can make something of her. Bring her," he said to the man at his side and turned his back. "We'll begin her training on the plane."

"Now hold on a minute—"

Sergei started toward her and Kat stepped back, looking for an escape. "I'm not going anywhere, and you can't make me."

"I can do exactly that," the monarch said, his expression dangerous. "I am your father. And your king."

Kat's knees quaked, but somehow she remained upright. "No. My father is dead. Mom told me—"

"Your mother lied." King Leopold raised his chin and narrowed his gaze, looking down on her. "You will come with me now and fulfill your duty. You will be announced as my successor in two weeks. As the future Queen of Bellevaux, there are naturally security concerns, so it's best we get you to the palace immediately."

Kat could barely breathe. "Security concerns?" Her mind whirled as the morning's events became clearer in her mind. "Like people coming after me, trying to kill me because I might be a stupid princess?"

Logan's words finally made sense. Kat turned on the king. "We were locked in that burning barn because of *you?*"

"You will be the next queen."

"No way. I gave up tiaras for cowboy boots when I was six. Find someone else to play dress up." Kat shoved Logan aside and stalked to her scuffed boots, propped against an elegant mahogany dresser. "I'm not putting my children's lives in danger for anyone."

"Children?" Both Logan and the king shouted at her.

Kat whirled around. "Yes. *My* children. And I need to get to them now. If a killer came after me, he could go after them, too."

Kat grabbed her Ropers and stuffed one foot in, then the other. She ignored her shaking hands. She had to get to Lanie and Hayden. She needed to see her kids, hug them, hold them, make sure they were okay. They were her family. Her *only* family.

Her eyes stung. She didn't need some father who didn't bother coming around until she was full grown, bringing danger into her life. She didn't need anyone.

She chanced a glance at Logan. His expression had turned stone still. She wouldn't have been able to recognize how badly her words had shocked him if she hadn't watched his index finger scratching against his thumb. She recognized the sign. She'd seen it the last time while she'd hidden from him. He'd come to her house right after she'd run. He'd cursed the empty building, then left. Kat had wanted to move, but she couldn't. She couldn't let herself hope.

A few months later she'd learned the hard way that she'd been right. Logan didn't really want her.

The king interrupted her thoughts.

"Your offspring. Do you have a son?" A small smile tilted his lips.

She didn't like the predatory gleam in his eye. "What does it matter? This facade is over. Go back where you came from, and leave me and mine alone."

She stalked to the door, grateful the sedative had worn off so she didn't resemble a drunk on a Friday night bar crawl.

"Stop her," the king ordered his flunky.

Sergei lunged at Kat. She stumbled away from him.

Logan stepped between them, cutting the man off. "I don't think so."

"You dare—"

"I dare a lot," Logan said. "Move away. Now."

Sergei didn't stop coming. Kat braced herself. She'd fight. For her kids. With a single swipe Logan laid the man on the ground with a Taekwondo move. Logan pressed his arm against the man's windpipe. "Don't think about crossing me. You won't win."

Sergei's eyes bugged out. He coughed and nodded his head.

Kat had never seen Logan this way. He was swift and deadly. She had no doubt he could maim or kill Sergei if he wanted to. The muscles in Logan's arms tensed as he pressed against Sergei's neck once more, then let him go with a warning glare.

"You've made your point," the king announced. "Which is why I didn't fire you when my son was murdered on your watch."

Kat gasped.

"Yes, young woman. Both of your half brothers were assassinated. Now do you see why you need protection?"

Kat's body went numb. "Logan?" She looked toward him, wanting nothing more than reassurance, but seeing none in his gaze.

"I'm sorry. You *do* need protection. This morning proves it."

She couldn't listen any longer. "We have to get my kids now."

"As my heir, you are coming with me," King Leopold commanded, his face and voice stubborn. "Logan, retrieve the children and meet me at the plane. We'll leave for Bellevaux at the earliest opportunity."

"No!" She'd fought too hard to take control of her life—for her and her children. She raced across the suite, yanked the door open and bolted down the hall.

"Kat!" Logan bolted after her, jamming the door to the suite. A spew of curses rose as Sergei and his men slammed against the wood. She didn't know how long it would hold.

Kat threw open the door to the stairwell. She had to get away. She'd go home, grab the twins and disappear. Someway, somehow. She'd never let her children around the man who *claimed* to be her father.

Heavy footsteps pounded after her, getting closer and closer. Within two flights Logan caught her by the arm and pulled her against him.

She shoved at his chest. "Let me go."

He pressed her to the wall. "Calm down. I just want to talk for one second. We need a quick plan."

She stilled. "We?"

"Yeah," he said, touching her cheek. "We."

"I'm not going with the king."

"We'll work something out, but you need to listen to me."

She gritted her teeth. "Why should I trust you? You drugged me."

"I didn't know about your children. If I had, I would have done things differently. I would have taken you to get them first." Logan dropped his forehead against hers. "Please, Kat. I won't let anything happen to you or them. I promise."

She took a deep breath. "You'll get me out of here?"

Logan lifted his head and met her gaze. "I'll find a safe place for you and your kids."

The truth of his words hung in the air between them. She finally nodded. She needed help.

He kept his Glock ready. "Let's go. We have to keep moving."

They raced down the stairs. "If the king finds us, you won't just hand over my kids?"

Logan stiffened beside her. "How could you ask me that?"

"I knew you for one week three years ago and you said you were a rancher, but you work for a king now."

"I *am* a rancher. One who's done some jobs for King Leopold over the years," Logan conceded. At the next level, he checked the small window to the hallway, before moving on. "I own a private investigation and security firm."

Kat's breaths came harder, but a flicker of hope glimmered. "Can you take us where I don't have to worry about him coming after us?" She grabbed his wool sweater. "I won't take any chances. Not with my children."

"I understand needing to protect your family, Kat." He helped her round the next level. "We'll have to make preparations. How old are your kids?"

Kat hesitated. She'd never thought to face this moment. Not after he'd had his ranch hands turn her away. "They're two and a half," she whispered softly, not wanting to meet his gaze, but knowing she had no choice.

Comprehension flashed across his face, and he tightened his grip on her arm. "They're mine?"

"I tried to tell—"

Above them, a door slammed open, and he cursed. "Save it. We need to get you out of here."

He grabbed her hand and pulled her down the stairs before she could argue. She'd tried to tell him when she'd found out. *He* was the one who hadn't wanted *her*.

When they reached the second to the last landing, a masked figure, pistol in hand, rammed through the door beside them. He aimed directly at Kat.

Logan tackled her and twisted his body to shield her. Both men's guns went off.

Logan sucked in a sharp breath. "Stay back," he snapped.

Faster than she could comprehend, he twisted his legs into a scissor lock around the assailant's knees and ankles and tripped him. The man tumbled down the stairs and slammed into the wall headfirst. Logan raced to follow, then stopped.

"Damn," he muttered.

The attacker stared sightlessly back, his neck at an unnatural angle.

Logan bent down and removed the balaclava that

masked the man's features, then swore. "This is one of Leopold's guards. I warned him he'd been infiltrated. If you'd gone with the king…"

"What if he'd gotten near the children?" She couldn't stop her voice from shaking.

Logan grabbed Kat's hand and pulled her to him. Kat huddled against Logan's chest, unable to stop trembling. *Please let this be a nightmare. Please let me wake up. Please let my babies be all right.*

Logan looked as if he wanted to say something, but he sighed and tapped his phone.

"Meet me at the back entrance. We're going to Plan B." A Russian curse sounded above them. "Sergei."

They hurried out the stairwell and around the corner.

"I'm late," Kat said. "I need to call my kids."

"You mean *our* kids?"

Kat nodded, a feeling of dread spreading inside her. "Yes. Our kids."

"You have one minute." He slipped a small metal tool into a locked maintenance closet door, closed them in and handed the phone over. She fumbled so many times he finally took the cell back.

"What's the number?"

Kat told him, then waited as he held the phone to his ear for a long time.

He hit a button and waited again.

"What's going on?"

Logan frowned. "It just keeps ringing. Do you have an answering machine?"

Her heart stopped. "Yes, but Paulina should have picked up by now. She's the babysitter and she wasn't planning on taking the kids out today."

"Well, the machine didn't answer and neither did anyone else."

THE THRONE ROOM WAS EMPTY.

It wouldn't be for long.

The double doors whispered open and cautious footsteps crossed the marble floors toward the spot where the duke stood admiring the way the gold-plated walls glistened.

He ignored the simpering fool behind him and continued his perusal.

After the redecoration in the wake of the recent massacre, this was now a room befitting his future plans for Bellevaux. No longer would it simply be a tourist destination wallowing in a glorious past. Countries would be courting Bellevaux's resources for the first time in a half century.

Rare earth metals were prized on the black market for weapon development. All he needed to take his place in Bellevaux's history were the right partners. The man who could parlay the metals into money had landed in his lap. His greater dilemma—a princess with a royal bloodline accepted by the people. Leopold's daughter was perfect, no matter how common. Once he had an heir off her, the American cowgirl could be disposed of. Everything was falling into place. As long as *he* maintained control.

"We have a problem, Your Grace."

The Duke of Sarbonne turned. "Did I grant you permission to speak, Niko?"

His advisor swallowed. "I beg your pardon."

"Very well." The duke nodded. "I'm beginning to believe our friends in America are not as competent as they claimed. Too many mistakes. Too long to gather information. Perhaps they have no stomach for what is required."

"There is news," Niko's voice rushed out. "The princess has children. One is rumored to be a boy."

The duke stilled.

"Your Grace?"

"Leave me," he snapped.

"As you wish." Niko bowed, his entire body shaking.

The doors whispered shut. The duke placed his hands behind his back and studied the exquisite tapestry from the Middle Ages depicting his ancestor in ruthless battle as that duke defeated his brother and seized the crown of Bellevaux. The sword the man had used hung prominently behind the throne now. Luminal would probably still reveal the ancient blood of those fools who sought to challenge.

Modern-day warfare required a different manner of weapon, but the duke intended the present outcome to be no less lethal. He retrieved his cell phone from his pocket.

"I assume you've heard about the…complications?"

"Yes, Your Grace. Or should I say Your *Majesty*."

"Soon." He liked the way the title sounded. Before too long, the entire country would embrace him as such. "Eliminate them, but the princess must live."

"Your Grace—"

"I told you, Victor, I need a princess. Take care of her illegitimate litter and you'll have all the rare earth metals you can mine."

"Then it will be done…Your Majesty."

"Victor, I'm not finished. Any mistakes, and I will be…disappointed." Sarbonne smiled at the memory of his morning's activities. "A state which has proved… most unhealthy…for others in the past."

Chapter Two

Logan pulled Kat around to the service elevator and punched the basement button. He didn't want to meet anyone else. One bullet wound near his shoulder was enough for now. Good thing it wasn't bad. He couldn't deal with first aid until later, so the cloth napkin he'd stolen off a breakfast tray would have to suffice for a bandage.

Logan's mind spun at the strange new truths shoved at him over the last few minutes. Kat was a princess. He was a father. No one was answering the phone where his children were supposed to be.

He had children.

Twins.

If he'd only known he could have sent a security team for them. He'd spent hours watching Kat sleep while horrible things could have been happening to his kids. The realization made him shake. He'd faced terrorists in Afghanistan and Iran, double agents who wanted him dead, and that didn't come close to his fear at the responsibility for two innocent lives. Lives he should have been protecting all this time.

The service elevator doors slid open and Logan pressed Kat behind him. He peered into the hallway, looking for Sergei, or rogue gunmen. Maids and kitchen staff bustled toward two large sets of swinging doors.

"This way," Logan said.

They followed a waiter and wove through the chaotic kitchen, then out through a delivery door.

Stepping into the bright winter sun behind the hotel, Logan's tension eased a fraction as a familiar black SUV with its window slightly down screeched to a stop in front of them.

Kat pulled back, her glimpse of the driver's stern visage and eye patch obviously scaring her.

"It's okay. Rafe's one of my best men."

The certainty in his words niggled at Logan's gut. He'd believed Daniel to be his closest friend and ally. Despite his trust, Logan had to keep his guard up.

He bundled Kat into the backseat and slid in beside her, his Glock on his lap. The darkened windows hid their identity, and he gave their surroundings a quick scan. Nothing tripped his alert wire. "Get us out of here fast, Rafe. Evasive maneuvers and keep your gun ready. I'm running red."

Logan met Rafe's intent gaze in the rearview mirror, but his right-hand man didn't hesitate or question how badly Logan was wounded.

Rafe pulled out, constantly checking the special mirrors set up to accommodate the temporary patch over his left eye. "Where to?"

Kat grabbed the seat in front of her. "We have to go to—"

Logan interrupted her. "Just lose anyone following us for now. We can't chance a tail."

At the stricken look in her eyes, his own stress surged. "Soon, Kat. This is a precaution for their safety, too. It'll just add a few minutes." His heart pounded at the thought of what could happen in a few minutes. Then again, if he led the killers to Kat's house, they'd all end up dead.

Logan's cell phone rang. He checked the number, not surprised to see the king's identification. Logan touched his earpiece. "I'm not bringing her to your hotel. I'll get back to you when I'm sure she's safe. By the way, if you're missing a bodyguard, he broke his neck in the hotel stairwell."

Logan ignored the tirade directed at him. "Yeah, well, your 'faithful servant' tried to kill Kat as we left. The background checks of your royal guards suck, Your Majesty. Think about that."

Logan ended the call and tapped another line.

"Hunter here."

Thank God. Logan couldn't have asked for a better operative to shadow the king. Hunter was on leave from an organization that was so far out of reach even the CIA couldn't pin them down. But his friend was based in Europe. He knew Bellevaux—and its politics.

"Keep the royal entourage in your sights. I need to know who's communicating with whom. Someone leaked our location. Twice."

His children's existence could have already made its way to the wrong people. Just the thought and Logan's stomach churned. If they'd been willing to burn Kat alive... He couldn't let himself think of worse possibilities.

"You want to bring the rest of your team in?" Hunter asked.

"No," Logan said. "Don't call anyone until I know where the mole is. For now, it's just you and Rafe."

"Got it. Hunter out."

Logan pocketed the cell, fighting the urge to call Kat's house again. He could see her trembling beside him, her eyes wide and fearful, her knuckles whitened. Did she realize—as the SUV twisted and turned through downtown Houston getting lost among the traffic until they reached the third ward—that Rafe was bringing them nearer to her house all the time?

Logan had found her address while she'd been sedated. Would it scare her that he knew where she lived? If he found it, surely those searching for her had, too.

Unable to resist, he tugged her hand from her lap. "We'll get there." He stroked her soft skin. She heaved a shuddering breath and nodded, her fingers relaxing slightly under his caress.

Rafe took another turn aiming toward the 601 loop. "No one is following us. Where to?" he asked, giving Kat a curious glance.

"Can I tell him?" she asked.

"Yeah, I trust him."

"But you don't trust all your men." She said it more as a statement of fact than as a question. "You just said as much to the man on the phone."

Logan hesitated, hoping she didn't hear about Daniel anytime soon. No need to worry her more than she already was. "I do trust them, and I don't think the leak is from my camp, but I'm not willing to take chances with our children's lives."

Logan met Rafe's shocked gaze in the rearview mirror for a half second, but that's all it took for the man to understand how much the stakes had changed.

Imperceptibly, the SUV sped up and headed in the right direction.

"The address?" Rafe asked again.

"Pasadena," Kat said quietly. She gave the location in a Houston suburb. They crossed south through some tough neighborhoods. Logan looked around, feeling his tension rise as he took in the sights. His kids were living in this area? Maybe in houses like these? Neighborhoods like these?

Places where walking to the grocery store could become a lesson in danger.

While he had a sprawling ranch, with dogs and horses and acres of land, and he lived the loneliest life a man ever had. All because Kat never told him he was a father.

Never gave him the chance to offer his kids something different.

Never gave *him* a chance to *be* something different...

Kat kept looking at him, waiting for him to speak and suddenly Logan didn't trust himself to say a word. If he opened his mouth he'd tear into her for the grief and betrayal she'd bubbled to the surface.

Women left men. They even left kids. He knew that.

Hell, it seemed to be a Carmichael family tradition to be walked out on.

He turned away from Kat, and a sharp pain sliced through his right shoulder. He hissed in a breath as the cloth rubbed across the bullet wound. Logan could feel it starting to bleed again. At least the dark leather would hide most of the blood.

"Are you okay?"

"I'm great." Logan rubbed the back of his neck and shifted again so Kat wouldn't see the bullet tear just above his shoulder blade. The wound wasn't bad, and he welcomed the pain. Better the one in his body than the one ripping through his heart.

"Logan—" she began.

"Don't, Kat. Not yet." He didn't know what to feel except that he had two kids out there who could be in danger and their mother had lied to him for three years. It's not like he'd kept his identity a secret. He'd told her about his ranch. She could have found him any time she wanted. Lived like the princess she apparently was in real life.

Kat straightened up when Rafe turned the car into an older neighborhood. The homes were well kept, though outdated, but his babies deserved better than this.

Logan's temper flared as he readied his Glock. Stupid blood loss was making him crazy, that was the problem. It was time to shape up and concentrate on the situation at hand. Volatile emotions weren't helping now. He had to remain cool, calm and rational.

The SUV pulled up to a small, wood-sided house.

Kat clutched at the door handle but Logan gripped the latch to keep her from opening it. "I'll go in first and make sure it's clear." He turned to Rafe. "Go around back and check things out."

"Got it." Rafe hopped from the vehicle.

Kat glared at Logan. "I'm going in. They're *my* kids."

"Get this straight, princess." He bit the words, holding a tight rein on his temper. "Those are my kids, too, and we're going to have one helluva talk about *that* once everyone's out and safe."

Kat's face paled, but Logan ignored it. Okay, so he'd blown cool and calm. Maybe he still stood a chance with rational.

He slipped out of the vehicle and took another deep breath. He had to maintain control, but dread churned in his gut. The house was dark and ominously still, with no sign that two active toddlers lived there. He didn't want to look at Kat right now. How could he forgive himself—or her—if something had happened to the twins?

He scanned the area, and when Rafe gave Logan a thumbs-up, indicating that the back of the house was clear, Logan opened the car door. "You can get out now, but stay with me."

She didn't argue, just hurried across the yard.

Logan kept vigilant as they reached the door. "It won't take long for the king to discover your address. He and his men are probably on their way."

She tugged keys from her jeans pocket and Logan took them from her.

"I go in first," he repeated as he unlocked the door. "I'll check the house, then you'll pack what the kids will need for a couple of days and go. Fast."

He pushed the door open and stepped into the small hallway. His stomach roiled. A sparsely decorated Christmas tree lay on its side, the homemade ornaments broken and scattered across the scarred wooden floor.

"What's the matter? Why are you stopping?" Kat shoved in beside him.

"Stay back."

"Oh, no." She clutched his arm. "Logan, where are my babies?"

He held her and she clawed at him, trying to get past.

"Be quiet. If they're still here, they'll hear you."

Tears of terror filled her eyes. Logan flicked his earpiece, signaling Rafe. "We have trouble. I need you inside."

In seconds, Rafe appeared behind them, his movements stealthy.

"Guard her," Logan said. "Don't let her follow me."

Despite her protests, Rafe firmly took Kat's arm. Logan turned away, his Glock ready. Slow and easy, he entered the house, his movements silent and careful. They were safe. Nothing was wrong. He repeated it like a mantra. Life couldn't be so cruel to take away the innocent children he hadn't met yet.

Kat moaned softly. "Hayden. Lanie."

Logan whipped his head around and held his finger to his lips.

She nodded, tears streaming down her face.

His entire body on alert, Logan rounded a corner and scanned the tiny kitchen. The remains of two tiny bowls of soup and a nearly finished grilled cheese sat on the table. Two small glasses of milk were half empty. He opened a sliding closet containing a stackable washer and dryer. Nothing. He eased down the hall checking out a small bathroom—clean and vacant. Only two more doors, both closed.

Logan put his ear to one. A grunt and sniffles sounded from behind it. His movements cautious, Logan eased it open, trigger finger ready.

A grandmotherly Hispanic woman sat in a rocker, her eyes closed, toys scattered all around the nursery. In a crib, a small girl lay sleeping, snuggled in a pink blanket. A towheaded boy hung over the edge of the crib, dangling. Before Logan could even speak the little one dropped to the floor, turned and stared up at Logan.

His eyes grew wide and serious. "Are you a bad guy?"

Logan blinked. "No."

"Why do you look scawy?"

Flummoxed, Logan scanned the closet, trying to concentrate on finishing the security check and not grabbing his son and holding him tight. "I'm looking for bad guys. Have you seen any?"

"No. Just you."

Logan turned back to find the kid holding a toy gun on him.

"Reach for the sky!"

Logan couldn't help it. He burst out laughing and lowered his weapon.

Paulina's eyelids flew open and she screamed, struggling to get out of the rocker.

So much for keeping things quiet.

"Clear," Logan called into the other room. "I'm not here to hurt you," he said softly to Paulina. "Kat's with me."

She raced into the room.

"Mommy!" The little boy leaped at Kat and she hugged him tight.

"How's my big boy?"

"I caught the bad guy—" he pointed to Logan "—wif my gun."

"Hayden, he's not a bad guy."

"He's not?" The little boy stared at Logan, a little disappointed. "He's on my side?"

Logan froze, his gaze meeting Kat's. "You bet. I'm definitely on your side."

"Hayden." Kat swept his blond hair off his forehead. "He's a very special man. He's your daddy."

Hayden turned around and glared at Logan. "Bad Daddy. Where'd you go? You're s'posta live with us."

KAT COULDN'T GET Logan's devastated expression out of her mind. Hurriedly, she zipped up her son's puffy blue coat while Hayden squirmed in her lap. Lanie, on the other hand, stood quietly, staring at Logan, her thumb in her mouth. Kat's daughter had an old soul. She watched everything. Unlike her brother who found trouble no matter how safe Kat tried to make things.

While Rafe patrolled outside, Logan stood guard at the window, his hand near his gun, his entire body alert and stiff. Tension vibrated in the room. Every look he gave her shot daggers, even while his expression softened and a smile tilted his lips when his gaze lingered on Hayden and Lanie.

"I'm so sorry, Katerina," Paulina repeated for the tenth time. "They're so…lively. They chased each other and Hayden rammed his fire truck into the tree. It just toppled over. I had hoped a nap would calm them. And me. The only time to rest is when they do."

"Believe me, I understand, Paulina. They're a handful." Kat pulled out her last twenty and placed it in the woman's hand. "Thank you for watching them. We'll be away for a few days."

"Longer." Logan strode over to Paulina. "Do you have someone you could visit out of town?"

The babysitter looked surprised. "I have a sister…in Mexico. Why?"

"It might not be safe in this neighborhood for a while." Kat didn't know what else to say without explaining too much.

"I cannot afford a visit," Paulina said, her look uncertain. "Do not worry. I'll be fine."

"Go see her." Logan handed her a thick envelope. "This will help. I never meant to scare you, and, after today, you could use a vacation. Merry Christmas."

Paulina opened the packet, shocked as she thumbed through the bills. She looked to Kat, who smiled and nodded her agreement. "Thank you," the woman said quietly. "I have missed *mi hermana*. It will be a good surprise to see her."

"Leave today." He gave Paulina a serious look and she agreed nervously. Logan picked up the kids' bags. "We need to hurry, Kat."

At his deep voice, Hayden twisted around. The boy couldn't stop looking at Logan. Kat understood. His intensity commanded attention, and despite their lives being in danger, Logan's presence made her feel protected and safe. But every cool glance flayed another layer of her heart open.

Kat grabbed a diaper bag from the floor and quickly added the three small stockings hung on the wall near the tree. Three. Not four. Would that change this year?

The babysitter hugged Lanie, then Hayden ran over and Paulina kissed the top of his head. "Goodbye, *niño*. Be good if you can."

She hugged Kat and hobbled out the door.

Hayden grabbed his white-and-red engine from next to the fallen Christmas tree. He raced over to Logan, stared at him, then offered him his treasured toy.

"I can't cawwy it to the car. You do it. Don't let the bad guys get it."

Kat's heart jolted at the gesture. "Logan, I think you've been forgiven."

She recognized the wonder in Logan's eyes as he whispered into his earpiece that they'd be out in a minute. Slowly he knelt to take the fire truck from his son. His movements were hesitant, wary, so very different from the certain, decisive moves he'd used against the men who'd attacked them.

"I'll make sure it gets to the car, Hayden."

"Me, too?"

"Yeah, buddy. You, too."

She'd known Logan as a sensual man and she'd seen him as a warrior today, but she'd never seen him like this…open…vulnerable…awed by a little boy's trust. He ran a trembling hand over her son's blond head. She'd never imagined Logan's touch could be so achingly tender. Kat swallowed back tears. She hadn't expected Logan to connect with Hayden so quickly—or to be so cautious with and amazed by Lanie.

Logan looked up and she pretended not to notice the sheen in his eyes, but she lost part of her heart to him then and there.

Or was that the part that had always been his?

"We need to leave now." His voice broke a bit.

She lifted the diaper bag with the stockings, then remembered the kids' presents. "Will we return in time for Christmas?"

"I don't know."

"Then I'll be right back." Kat handed Lanie over to Logan and raced into her bedroom.

She tugged a small bag from her closet, filled with a few toys and clothes she'd collected at yard sales over the summer. It wasn't much, but at least they'd have something for Christmas. She hurried back to the living room where a panicked Logan held their screaming daughter, tears raining down her face. Hayden ran in circles around them.

Logan tried rocking Lanie, his movements awkward, but she just wailed louder. "She won't stop."

Rafe knocked on the door, then stepped inside. "Hunter called. Sergei and three men are heading this way. ETA fifteen minutes."

"Take the bags and put them in the SUV," Logan ordered Rafe.

His certain tone stopped Lanie's tears. She blinked up at him.

Logan stroked her cheek. "You like your men more decisive, huh? Okay, we're out of here."

She cocked her head sideways and plopped her thumb in her mouth.

He held out the baby to Kat, who had grabbed a kicking Hayden. "Trade you."

"Gladly." She took Lanie, and they ran out the door. "We need car seats."

"Done. Rafe put them in the backseat." An identical SUV idled behind the black monstrosity Rafe had driven.

She sent him a questioning glance.

"Decoy." He put Hayden into the backseat, nearly smacking his son's head on the underside of the roof in his rush, then fumbled with the latches. "These are not meant for fast getaways, and we're out of time."

Kat shoved him aside. "Give Hayden his toy. I'll do it."

She settled the kids and slid into the front seat. Her heart raced. "How far away are the king's men now?"

"Ten minutes."

Logan quickly pulled out and took an indirect route back to the highway. He glanced at the kids. Hayden's eyes had closed almost as soon as they started driving.

"He's already asleep?"

"Hayden has two speeds. Dangerous and comatose."

Lanie snuggled with her blanket and stared out the window at the passing winter landscape. Eventually, her head started to nod, too.

Logan turned the SUV north on a secondary road, leaving the heavy Houston area traffic behind. Despite frequent mirror checks, he became increasingly edgy.

After a few miles of silence, his knuckles had turned white. "Why didn't you tell me you were pregnant?" he asked. "I could have been here to help you before this. I could have protected the twins and you."

"Don't put that on me, Logan," she whispered, the past hurt peeling away at her heart. "*You* sent me away."

He shook his head. "That's not the way I remember

it. You left a note at the hotel! A damn note—" Logan looked over his shoulder at the kids.

Lanie stared back, her eyes bright with tears.

He lowered his voice. "A note that said nothing. You vanished, Kat. I tried to find you. I tracked down where you used to live. You'd quit your job, left your apartment. You went into hiding. What was I supposed to think? *Please, Logan, keep looking for me?*"

Lanie reacted to the tension in the car and whimpered, her bottom lip quivering.

Kat glanced back at their children. "Logan, please, we can't do this now."

"You're right," he said, staring into the rearview mirror. "We have company."

"What?" She whipped around. A large SUV barreled up behind them.

Logan sped up, but the other vehicle matched their speed then slammed into the back with a jolt. Hayden and Lanie cried out in fear. Logan held the steering wheel tight and somehow managed to keep them on the road.

Everything in Kat called to comfort her kids, but saving their lives came first. She squinted through the back windshield. "I can't see who it is," she said. "Their windows are tinted."

Her entire body shook with anger. Her children were innocent. She gripped Logan's arm. "What can I do?"

He looked at her, a flash of approval in his eyes. "A van just cut them off. Switch places with me before they catch up again. I'll try to take them out from the backseat."

Logan shoved the center console up so they could maneuver across the bench seat. He scooted from behind the wheel. Kat unhooked her seat belt, scrambled over him and took control.

"Floor it," he said, lifting his foot from the accelerator. He bent down and pulled a military-looking rifle from beneath the seat. He shoved a clip into it and pocketed a second.

The truck rammed them again. The kids screamed louder.

"Hayden, Lanie, there's going to be some loud noise and bangs so we're going to hide. Okay?" Kat said.

Hayden curled over his truck, then looked at his sister. "We playing seek and go hide," he whispered. Lanie put her thumb in her mouth and curled down like him.

"They're amazing," Logan said as he reached over her to flip a switch. The back window rolled down partway while Logan crawled over the second seat and into the back.

Hayden popped his head up to watch his father. "Daddy gots a big gun!"

Kat's stomach dropped at her son's curiosity. She struggled to keep the vehicle on the road and maintain her cool—for the kids' sake.

"Hide, Hayden. Hide for Mommy."

Hayden rolled up into a small ball. "Daddy 'tect you, Lanie. Don't be ascared."

Kat wanted to hold them in her arms, but she couldn't. Her gaze swept back to the road and she gasped. She bore down on a slow-moving station wagon and swerved around it. A semi barreled toward them. Her heart lurched and she screeched back into her lane. The truck blared its horn.

"Keep it steady," Logan yelled over the icy winter wind whistling through the vehicle. "They're coming up fast."

Bullets sprayed from his rifle. The kids cried out in

terror. Smoke billowed from the engine of the car chasing them and it whirled off the side of the road.

"You did it." Kat eased her foot off the gas. "We escaped."

"Temporary reprieve," Logan said. "Roll up the window."

He climbed into the backseat. With gentle hands he comforted his screaming children. "You're okay now. I'm sorry for the bad noise. It's gone." He hugged them close and closed his eyes, rocking them until only hiccups and sniffles remained. "It's okay. Don't be scared. Daddy's got you."

Kat swallowed back a tumult of emotions.

Finally, after a few minutes, Hayden squirmed. "Too much hugging."

"Sorry, little buddy."

"I like it," Lanie said, and buried her face into Logan's chest.

He kissed their cheeks and adjusted them in the car seats. His jaw tight, he snagged his phone from his pocket and tapped it. "Rafe, I left you a mess on highway 34. Take care of it."

Logan drummed his fingers on the seat back while he listened to Rafe's response. "We're being tracked somehow, and if that wasn't the king's men, things are worse. I'm dumping the vehicle. I'll be in touch when I can. Find the leak that's making it possible for these people to find us."

Kat brushed the tears of relief from her eyes and swallowed as this new reality hit her. She met Logan's gaze as he closed the phone. "Is this latest leak in the king's camp or yours?"

"I don't know," he acknowledged, "but until I find out, we're on our own."

PAULINA PEERED OUT the curtain and stared at the black SUV and the terrifying man with the patch over one eye. He hadn't moved from in front of Katerina's house. Why was he staying there? *La familia* was gone with the other man with the gun. So many scary people. She wouldn't babysit in that house anymore. She was even afraid in her own house now. What if someone learned what she'd done?

Paulina's hands trembled and she twisted her shawl, unraveling the stitches. A chilling fear had gone through her when the big man warned her of danger and demanded she leave today. She still couldn't get warm. Maybe she *should* go to her sister's house. They wouldn't follow her across the border. Would they?

She hurried toward her bedroom to pack, but she'd only made it partway when the back door slammed open.

Paulina trembled with fright.

A huge man entered her living room, his face red with anger, blood staining his right shoulder.

"Who are you? Please go. I have no money," she lied.

"You should. I paid you, but you failed me."

Paulina gasped. She recognized the voice. The phone call she hadn't been able to ignore. "But I...I...did what you wanted. You said you would leave me alone."

"Well, they escaped. And someone has to pay."

"Please, don't hurt me." She glanced at the bloody shirt. "I'll take care of your wound. I won't tell anyone."

"Sorry, but I've been shot and the family got away. They will die, and you're the only one who can tie me to them."

Paulina backed toward the window, and the giant smiled, his expression evil. He pulled a huge, serrated knife from a leather sheath wrapped around his leg. He slid his thumb along the shiny blade.

Paulina gulped, her heart galloped, skipping beats. Her head swam and she swayed. "Please, no," she whimpered. "I'll be silent."

"Yes," he said softly and raised the blade. "You will."

Chapter Three

Logan stayed in the backseat with the kids, his rifle loaded in case of another ambush. He hadn't recognized the other SUV or the shooters, but they'd been out to kill the entire family. And they'd been tailed too easily. Only one possibility. There had to be a tracking device.

Hayden clung to one arm, Lanie to the other, their small bodies pressed up against Logan. His heart swelled with an all-encompassing need to care for and protect them. He smiled down at them, and they blinked up, their tear-streaked faces caging his soul. They had him. He'd do anything for them.

He studied the terrain. Before the vehicle went much farther, he needed to do a sweep. He hated to risk stopping, but he didn't think their attackers would quit after one attempt. He wouldn't make it easy for whoever followed them.

Several miles passed before he identified a relatively safe stopping point.

"Pull over," he ordered Kat.

"Here?" She gave him a shocked look.

"Now," Logan insisted. "Take us behind those birch trees. Out of sight of the highway."

She turned down a dirt road, gripped the wheel tightly and guided them over the bumps and deep ruts.

Logan hated to move. He'd been in heaven, holding his children against him. He hadn't known what to expect, but even though they'd known him only a few hours, they burrowed against him. They apparently trusted him a lot more than their mother ever had.

He met Kat's gaze in the rearview mirror briefly. Every second with his children raised his frustration with her. It shouldn't be this way.

Lanie stirred beside him as Kat eased the car into a hidden spot. The little girl was a strange creature, so delicate. He'd felt like an oaf holding her. He was a guy. He understood Hayden and his daredevil instincts, but this fragile baby? He worried he'd break her. Maybe if he'd been there from the start it would be different, but he'd missed everything. He'd make it up to the twins, though. That, he promised.

He didn't know what to do with Kat, except save her life. Trusting her wasn't going to come easy.

The SUV rolled to a bumpy stop, startling Lanie from sleep. Her wide eyes met his gaze in panic. "It's okay, sweetie. Daddy's got you."

She patted him. "Daddy," she whispered.

Hayden, on the other hand, looked like he'd had enough.

"Down," he ordered, his expression mutinous.

His kid was right. Logan had to move quickly.

"Why are we stopping?" Kat asked, shifting in her seat.

"I'm checking the SUV for bugs. Get them out of their car seats."

He passed Lanie to Kat then lifted Hayden. As he did, he caught the whiff of a distinctly toxic odor. "Whoa." Logan stared at Hayden as recognition hit. "You wear diapers?"

"Good thing for us or we'd be stopping every ten minutes. They're not potty trained," Kat said, biting her lip, but humor danced in her eyes. "They're *considering* it."

Logan clutched his squirmy son. The imp just grinned at him, tugged at the waist of his small jeans and started pushing them down his legs.

"Uh, Kat. He's taking his clothes off." Logan fought to keep his son from undressing but within seconds Logan had clearly lost the battle. As much as he wanted to ignore Kat's laughter, he was way out of his league here. Give him a bomb that needed disarming, a grenade launcher or room full of terrorists any day over these two.

He shot her an exasperated look. "Take him. I'll learn the intricacies of diaper changing later. For now, I need to check out the SUV's rear end, not Hayden's."

Logan leaped out of the car and sucked in a breath of fresh air. Man, the kid was ripe. Logan yanked the tailgate, but it wouldn't budge. He moved to the front and turned the key, rolling down the back window as far as the damaged back allowed.

"What are you looking for?" she asked, as she quickly changed both kids, then sat them down on a blanket with juice boxes and a snack.

"My equipment bag. I have a bug sweeper in there. Those men knew where we were," he said. "I need to check for a transmitter."

He rounded the SUV and reached in. Part of his duffel was caught in the crumpled metal of the rear tailgate and it had been littered with bullets. Great. He unzipped the bag and rifled through its contents. The case containing his electronic detector had been decimated. Holding his breath, he pulled out the shot-up equipment. The bug detector was beyond hope.

He grabbed his phone, another link to the outside world. Supposedly secure. Only his computer expert, Zane, should be able to trace his location with it.

Logan hesitated. His gut told him to remain incommunicado. He pulled the battery from the phone and unhooked the GPS power source. He wasn't taking any more chances. Not with his kids' lives.

He looked over at them. Each child sipped on a juice box while Kat sang softly to keep them entertained. He wanted to watch and listen, but they couldn't afford to stay anywhere for long. He needed to find that transmitter. Nothing else explained how the gunmen had found them.

Logan rifled through the equipment, searching for anything out of place then checked the kids' seats before beginning a swift visual search on the vehicle's exterior.

"What are you doing now?" Kat asked. "I thought you had a detector."

"It's ruined. That makes us vulnerable." He rose quickly and dusted off his jeans. "Get everything else out of the SUV, Kat. Fast. If we don't absolutely have to have it, we're dumping it and getting the hell out of here."

Logan stripped the vehicle of anything not nailed down except for his most sensitive high-tech equipment, the diaper case and one toy each to distract the kids. He grimaced at Kat's dismay as she dumped a garbage bag of clothes and toiletries, but when he grabbed the small bag from the floor of the backseat and threw it on the trash pile, she clutched his arm.

"No," she hissed. "Those are Christmas presents. It's all they'll have. Please don't."

At her desperation, Logan stopped and peered inside. A used train and doll lay alongside two tiny packaged toys and one outfit for each child. His knuckles whitened on the bag as he viewed the meager items. He'd known money was tight for Kat, but this? He raised his head. Embarrassment laced her gaze. Silently, he checked the toys out and handed her the bag. She clutched it, looking away.

He wanted to comfort her, but what could he say?

He slid under the car and, using telescoping mirrors, checked the undercarriage, front to back. After a few minutes, he cursed. "Gotcha."

He showed her the bug, then smashed it. "Okay, we're out of here. They could be close by for all we know."

They buckled the kids into the car, but remained silent. For a brief few moments earlier, they'd experienced the initial ease that had existed between them three years ago. From the moment they'd first met, they couldn't stop talking or touching each other. Being with her then had felt so natural. Now, the awkward silence made his chest ache.

Logan forced his mind from the past and quickly covered the pile of equipment and Kat's belongings with dead branches and leaves. She stared at the mound, then, without speaking, climbed into the passenger's seat. Holding herself stiffly, she peered out at the flat landscape beyond the birch trees.

Sighing, Logan took one look at his sleepy children and started the vehicle. He waited until the kids had finally nodded off before broaching the subject he'd wanted to talk about for hours. "I would have helped you any way I could, if you'd just come to me."

Her eyes flashed with anger and residual embarrassment. "I did come to you."

"When?"

"Once I found out I was pregnant, I tracked you down. I came to your ranch and pleaded to see you.

Your men wouldn't even let me through the gate. They said you were *indisposed* and nothing I said would get you to talk to me." Pain punctuated every word. "After that heartwarming welcome, I didn't have to be told twice that you didn't want me around."

Logan looked at her in shock. "I never turned you away."

"So what? I'm lying?" she shot back. "You think I would make up a story about going to your ritzy ranch in Carder, Texas?"

He glared at her. "*You* don't exactly have a great track record for reliability and honesty, Kat. Point in fact—me meeting my kids for the first time today."

She flinched, but then her jaw tightened. "I don't lie. I hate liars. Do you want proof I went to you that day? You want me to describe the entrance to your ranch? The iron gates with the horseshoe? The horses and cattle? My walk from the bus station? Or maybe you want the original bus ticket I purchased as proof that I bought it. Sorry, I try not to hold on to unhappy memories, of which you were my biggest one *ever*, Logan Carmichael." Her breath came fast and furious.

Dead silence fell over the car.

Fuming, hurt and confused as hell, Logan turned his full attention back to the road, struggling to make sense of it all. Her anger seemed too real, too visceral. Could she be telling the truth?

The miles passed and only the gentle breathing of the two sleeping children broke through the thick silence.

"You weren't my most unhappy memory, Kat," he said quietly. "Not at first."

She brought her head up in surprise.

"We made love all night long, then *you* left *me*. Remember?"

God knows Logan did. He'd held her close and confided to her about his dreams, of making his ranch more than his mother ever believed possible before she'd vanished when he was thirteen. He'd laid open his heart to Kat. He'd spoken of the future and they'd drifted off to sleep wrapped in each other's arms.

Once morning light hit, her sheets had gone cold.

"I searched for you," he said. "I came to your house."

"I know." She twisted her fingers.

"What?"

"I saw you." She paused. "I was coming home from the store. You were going up the stairs. I noticed your expensive car. The nice clothes and...I hid."

"From me? Why? Why did you run in the first place?"

She fidgeted in her seat, toying with the seat belt, gazing anywhere but at him. "I was afraid. Everything had been so magical. I knew it couldn't last. Then, when you talked about your ranch, I looked it up on the hotel computer. I saw your beautiful spread. I grew up on the wrong side of the tracks with nothing. I knew I'd never fit into your world. I was afraid if I fell for you, and you realized that, I would be left behind, like my mother was. I knew you deserved more than I could offer someone like you. You proved me right when you turned me away."

"What a crock." He glared at her. "You know nothing about my life or how I grew up. My father was an alcoholic and nearly drove the ranch into the ground. He gambled away half the acreage that had been in my mother's family for five generations. I begged, borrowed and stole to keep the place running. I thought I saw something special in you. I never would've rejected you."

Kat sank back into her seat and shook her head. "But your men did. I figured you told them not to let me in."

Logan paused. "When...exactly...did you try to get onto the ranch?"

"January fourth. Almost three years ago," she said. "Not a visit or a day I'll ever forget."

Logan let out a loud curse and rubbed the scar just above his temple. "Three years ago. Kat, for most of December and January I was in a German hospital... in a coma."

"Coma?" Kat's words were dazed.

She placed her hand near his, her fingertip following the ridge of skin leading into his hair. Logan's breath caught at her caress. He clasped her hand.

"What happened?" she whispered.

"Ambush," he said, not revealing his distraction on that mission, his constant thoughts of her.

"You weren't there," she said softly, as if trying to wrap her brain around the past. "They weren't lying." She tilted her head back and gazed at the roof of the car. "They could've explained. They could have told me you were in a hospital, or out of the country."

"My employees have strict orders never to reveal my location to anyone." He kneaded the knotting muscles at the back of his neck. He could see how it could have happened.

She'd tried to find him to tell him about the kids. She'd hadn't abandoned him, and he was as guilty for their not being together as she was. Worse, he'd lied to her. She'd been an assignment when he'd tracked her down—then and now. He'd felt the connection then. It had never died.

After she'd left, a small part of him had wondered if he'd lost his touch at reading people. In the CIA, he'd always had to trust his instincts. He'd have been dead a dozen times over if he didn't. But ever since the mother he adored walked out on him without saying goodbye, he'd never completely relied on blind faith again. Until the week with Kat.

She'd eviscerated him when she left. He couldn't believe she'd come back—unlike his mom. "Did you leave your name or a message for me before you left?" If she had, he'd be raking someone over the coals when he got back to the ranch.

"No. I was too angry and hurt." She exhaled in frustration. "Then again, they didn't ask me for anything."

"They probably figured you'd get in touch with me later. If it was important."

"All the nasty thoughts and horrible suspicions I had about you now seem so petty and insignificant. What a waste of time and possibilities. I've hated you for three years." Pure heartbreak tinged Kat's voice.

"Ditto." But the heavy weight he'd been carrying lifted from Logan's chest. He'd felt tired before, but suddenly he had a burst of energy. He could breathe again fully for the first time in forever.

She rubbed her eyes. "What do we do now?"

"We try to move past it." He turned his head to the sleeping children. "For them."

"All I want is a better life, but between the king and whoever else is chasing us, the whole world is off-kilter." Kat let out a long slow breath and leaned back against the seat. "What's going to happen to us, Logan? I can't run from these people the rest of my life. How will I protect my babies?"

"I have the best men in the business looking to find out who's after you. I *will* keep you and the kids safe."

"Can't I just tell that man, 'no,' and make this princess problem go away?"

"It's not that easy," Logan said grimly. "Bellevaux is

a very traditional country. Bloodlines mean everything. You carry the king's blood. So do our children. If he doesn't designate you or one of the children as his heir, you and your family will always be a threat to whomever ascends the throne."

"Even if we renounce any claim?" Desperation tinged her voice.

"Some won't take the risk of you changing your mind."

"Then they won't stop until we're dead. They can't."

The matter-of-fact words chilled Logan's soul. He reached out his hand and held hers tight. "We'll find a way to work this out."

He prayed he wasn't lying.

NERVES STRETCHED TO breaking, Kat gripped Logan's hand, needing the reassurance of his touch, terrified by the idea that others might want to kill her and the kids, no matter what she said or did. Logan stroked her palm with his thumb, his touch calming. Nothing seemed to faze him.

He kept checking the rearview mirror, but so far he seemed to believe that they weren't being followed. Still, he took evasive maneuvers and doubled back to make sure.

"I can't believe this is happening. I just wanted to finish nursing school and take care of my kids."

"Is that why you were only working with horses at Daughtery's ranch on the weekends? Because of school?"

She rubbed the calluses on her right hand, knowing they were both talking about this subject to avoid the far more troubling ones. "I spent the weekends teaching riding lessons, training horses and mucking out stalls so I could go to nursing school during the week."

"But why nursing school, Kat?" he asked, sounding honestly curious. "You're the best I've ever seen at gentling a horse. You could've been doing it professionally."

Heat stained her cheeks and she shook her head in denial. Maybe she had a way with horses, but she was certainly nothing special.

Logan flicked on the turn signal to take the next exit ramp. "Why are you embarrassed? You're gifted."

"Gifted doesn't pay for day care or sending my kids to college. Nursing will. It'll give them more than I had."

"I'm here now. That won't be a problem anymore."

"I can't let you take care of us. I ran from you because I was afraid to step out of my little world. Having Hayden and Lanie made me want to do something important with my life. I wanted to show them that there's more out there if you work hard enough. I struggle every day to keep believing that, terrified I can't make it happen, no matter what I do. I want them to have everything, Logan. Everything this world could possibly offer."

"The king could offer you more money than you ever dreamed and ruling a country is certainly important."

"It's not the same. I can't go with him, Logan. I'm no princess. I can't do what he wants me to do. Besides, you heard him. My father really only wants Hayden. Lanie and I are expendable. I won't have Lanie believing she doesn't matter. That price is too high."

He reached out and stroked her cheek. "You're an amazing woman, Kat."

She leaned into his caress, taking the comfort and strength he offered.

"My mother died feeling betrayed by him. She may have lied about who I was, and not told me he was still alive, but she spoke the truth about how she felt. He crushed her spirit. That will never happen to Lanie or Hayden."

"If you don't want to go with him, Kat, you don't have to."

"Unless it's the only way to keep the kids alive." The truth terrified her. "Money and power like his are hard to fight."

He shocked her when he pulled to the side of the road, out of sight of the passing cars, and cupped her face in his hands.

"Katherine Nelson. I watched you today. You're strong enough to deal with anything. If you don't want to go to Bellevaux, then don't go, but I refuse to listen to you give up. You're better than that. We'll find a way out of this together."

He didn't understand. Everything in her wanted to reach out to him, to lean into his strength, but she couldn't.

Logan unclicked his seat belt and leaned closer. He stroked her cheek, his touch caring, his eyes gentle.

She tilted her head into his warmth and stilled as his breath caught in a way she remembered from years before. His hazel eyes flared with green, darkening with a familiar arousal as if he remembered, too.

"What are we doing?" she asked, her voice barely above a whisper.

"I don't know." His gaze dropped to her lips and he threaded one hand through her hair and drew her closer.

Heat flared within her. She knew his touch, his kiss, the way he made her cry out his name in the dark. She'd dreamed of feeling like this again too many nights to admit.

The pad of his fingertip caressed her bottom lip. The rough texture made her shiver and she couldn't resist.

Her tongue tasted him and she drew his fingertip into her mouth. A groan rumbled deep inside his chest. His gaze held hers captive.

This was insane. They were on the run. They needed to go, but her entire body shook with awareness, while deep within her belly she softened, craving the feel of him pressed up against her, the caress of his lips and his hands as he explored every inch of her skin.

He tugged her closer, pressing her breasts against his chest. His lips hovered over hers, teasing, tempting. Kat lifted her mouth to his and gave in to the desire. Logan wrapped her in his arms and took over the kiss. Her heart raced, reveling in his power and passion.

She sighed against his mouth. He drove away the ugly frightening world that threatened them. For one moment it was only him and her and the memories of the surf pounding in rhythmic counterpoint as they sought release with each other.

"Why are you kissing Mommy?" Hayden piped up from the back.

Kat froze. She didn't want to let Logan go. She dragged her lips from his and looked at her son in disbelief. "When did you wake up?"

"When you and Daddy started making funny noises." Hayden reached for his fire truck and turned the siren on, waking up Lanie, who started crying. "I'm hungry. I want macaroni."

"Kid sure knows how to kill a moment, doesn't he?" Logan muttered, his fingertip caressing her lower lip, his gaze heated with promises for later. He slid the car back into Drive.

She tried to smile. Maybe Hayden's interruption had been for the best. She'd been ready to combust in Logan's arms. She took a shuddering breath and ordered her pounding heart to slow.

"Do we dare stop and get something to eat?" asked Kat.

"I'll find something out of the way. Since I identified that bug, we can probably spare twenty minutes. I just want to get to the ranch and lock everything down."

Pink and blue streams decorated the horizon at dusk as Logan pulled into a small diner in a town too similar to most of those Kat and her mom had lived in. One stop sign, a restaurant, a feed lot and a gas station doubling as a grocery store.

"I don't want to do this again for a while, but we need food, a few supplies and more than that, we need to ditch this SUV. The gunmen know the license plate and with the back smashed, it's too easy to spot."

"Is Rafe meeting us?"

"Not until I get a disposable phone. I saw a sign at the gas station about a car lot. I figure, even with damage, someone there will trade vehicles with us. They're going to have to buy it for scrap though. I don't want anyone driving the SUV on the road in case it eventually gets tracked down and the gunmen shoot first and ID the occupants later."

Kat shuddered. "I hadn't even considered. They're that desperate?"

"Maybe. And maybe they're just getting paid very, very well."

"Your world is frightening," Kat said with a frown. She studied the beat-up station wagon and several old pickups in the parking lot of the diner with new eyes. None of them looked suspicious. "Should we order our food to go?"

He shut off the vehicle. "You and the kids eat fast,

while I get the supplies and trade in the SUV. I don't like being apart, but the fewer people that see us together, the better."

Kat clutched Lanie close, emotion catching in her throat. Anyone who did see the four of them together would think they were a normal family. Little did they know that Logan and Kat were virtual strangers who may not live until tomorrow.

She followed Logan into the diner and they sought out the most secluded booth possible near the back. Within moments he'd ordered a spread of chicken nuggets and macaroni and cheese, quick fare that both kids would eat. After strapping Lanie into her high chair, Logan bent close to Kat's ear. "I'll be right back. If you see anything suspicious, run. I'll meet you out back."

She held his hand tight. "You'll be careful?"

His eyes crinkled. "Don't you worry. I've done this before."

She watched him walk out, confident, certain and oh-so-sexy in those jeans. She shouldn't be thinking that way, but Logan's intelligence and resourcefulness made her want him all the more. She survived. He planned— and won.

By the time the waitress delivered their meal, Logan had returned with new keys in his hand.

"I traded for the station wagon. They're going to sell the SUV for parts," he whispered. "I told them to keep it out of sight. From the looks of the place, by tomorrow, the SUV won't exist."

"Good. Now no one gets hurt," she muttered.

Logan's smile melted away. "I couldn't risk that." Logan glanced at his watch. "We should get on the road. Are the kids almost done?"

"Yes." Kat placed her hand on his for a moment. "You're a good man, Logan Carmichael."

He turned his hand over and held hers tight. "I missed you, Kat. I wish things had gone differently."

She held her breath.

He ran his thumb over her sensitive skin. "Do you think, once this is over, we could try—?"

"Mommy! Look! I opened the belt." Hayden climbed onto the table. "Vrooom!" He drove his fire engine through the chicken nuggets, then over his sister's hand. Lanie screamed and Hayden dove onto the bench seat, then under the table.

"Hayden. You come up here and apologize to your sister," Kat ordered.

Logan bent across to wipe Lanie's tears and in seconds, Hayden had scrambled out from his hiding place and bolted across the small, nearly empty diner, heading for the door.

"Hayden," Logan's deep voice warned.

Her son stopped and stared, obviously unsure of just how much he could get away with around this new "daddy."

The waitress did not look thrilled about a little kid running around the restaurant. Nor did the few patrons eating there.

Logan stood. "You stay with Lanie. I'll get him."

Logan strode toward Hayden, but Kat recognized the mischievous glint in her son's eye. "Hayden, no!" She bolted toward him.

Grinning, Hayden crouched down, ready to run. "Come get me, Daddy!"

In the few seconds it took for Logan and Kat to cross the distance, Hayden had scrambled onto the bench seat beside the door, then onto the top. Logan caught Hayden before he sailed through the front glass window, but his fire engine flew from his hands and smashed on the ground. Several pieces littered the linoleum floor.

Stunned, Logan sat on the bench seat, clutching his frustrated little boy. They both stared at the damaged toy. Kat could scarcely breathe, knowing it could just as easily have been Hayden lying there.

He wriggled and got down, then crawled to the fire engine. The ladder and one set of wheels had come off. "Broken, Daddy. Fix it," he pleaded, tears in his eyes, as he walked back and put the remains in his father's hands.

Kat stood beside them, now with a tearful Lanie in her arms.

Logan turned the fire truck over, then stilled as he saw gouge marks on the metal near one of the seams that the now-missing ladder had covered. He grabbed a knife from the table, slipped it into the seam and popped a compartment open.

Cursing, he grabbed Hayden and then their bags. "Come on, let's go."

"What's wrong?"

He threw some bills on the table. "I found another transmitter. Somehow they planted it in Hayden's toy. That means they know we're here."

Kat's heart pounded as they raced out the door. They quickly latched the kids into the car seats Logan had placed in the back of the station wagon, then jumped into the front. Logan screeched out of the diner's parking lot and got on the road. Once on the highway, he looked for a truck stop with an easy-on, easy-off access.

He pulled up to some construction vehicles and bent underneath the rear fender of the cement mixer.

"What are you doing and why are we heading back toward Houston?"

"We're not. But this transmitter is going the opposite way from where we are headed. The gunmen will know we're not all in this cement mixer, so the driver should be safe."

He hopped back in the car and drove away. A half hour later, he stopped again and dialed a number on one of the new disposable phones. After it connected, he punched in another series of numbers, then waited.

"Rafe, it's me. Where's Sergei? Did he ever show up?" Logan was silent as he listened, then his knuckles went white.

Kat trembled. Something was very wrong.

"They've gone too far. We're headed back to the ranch. Call everyone in. We'll pool our resources and end this thing."

He threw the phone on the seat and took several deep breaths. The acid in Kat's stomach churned. The anger pulsing off him was palpable. The warrior was back. Cold. Ruthless. Determined.

Frightening.

"What happened?" Kat could hear the terror in her own voice. Whatever it was, it had to be awful to put this deadly look in Logan's eyes.

"It's Paulina." Logan turned, his expression sad and regretful. "Someone got to her first. They hurt her. Bad."

"But she was leaving," Kat insisted. "Going to her sister's house. Is she okay?"

"I'm sorry, Kat. She's dead."

Chapter Four

Moonlight danced along the blacktop as Logan pulled up to the electronic gate leading to his family's ranch house. He keyed in his override code and rubbed his burning eyes as the gate swung open. He tried to imagine Kat standing here, pregnant and afraid, feeling that he'd rejected her, didn't want anything to do with her. That couldn't have been further from the truth.

He put the station wagon in gear and started down the long winding road to his house. He looked up at the imposing edifice, comparing it to where Kat and the kids had been living. Would the massive ranch house scare her all over again, or did the hitmen coming after her make his place look like a haven now?

He eased the car to a stop in front of the porch. The seven-hour drive had taken closer to ten, and all his muscles were stiff. The gunshot wound across his shoulder ached, but the bleeding had stopped.

He slid a sidelong glance at Kat. She was still sound asleep, the shadows under her eyes having grown dark, the worry pulling at the corners of her mouth. His hand hovered over her cheek. She was so damn beautiful.

He couldn't believe he'd told her he missed her. He'd never meant to say it out loud, but it just spilled out. He didn't want to be a fool for her again, but she seemed able to reach inside him and fill this big empty space with just the sound of her laughter—or the sight of her holding his babies.

Gently, he shook her awake. "Honey, we're home."

Damn, there he went again. He hoped she overlooked the slip.

Kat stirred, then sat up slowly. "Home?" She looked around sleepily. "You mean your ranch?"

She stared at the big house and he could almost see the nervousness take hold of her as she straightened in the seat.

"You'll be safe here." His heart ached with the need to pull her against him and make all her fears go away, but nothing would be that easy. He sighed, opened the car door and grabbed a few bags, setting them on the landing, knowing help would arrive soon.

Rafe met him on the front porch. "You took your time getting here."

"I had to dump the second transmitter in the back of a cement truck heading east. Hopefully, the decoy will keep them busy for a while," Logan said quietly, walking with Rafe to the car. Logan opened the back door of the station wagon and removed his daughter from her car seat. "I also doubled back a lot to make certain I wasn't followed."

"I noticed you ditched *our* phone transmitter, too. Zane was pissed when he lost track of you. Gotta tell you, Logan, a commando geek thinking you don't trust his security is *not* a pretty sight."

"He'll have to get over it," Logan said under his breath. "I couldn't risk anyone tapping into our signal and tracking us while I was on the road. That station wagon doesn't have near the horsepower of my SUV, and those kids have been through enough."

"That's why he was freaking." Rafe didn't wait to be asked what needed to be done. He walked around the other side of the car and picked up the dead weight of Hayden.

The day's events must have worn the kids out. Neither woke.

For a moment, Kat lingered beside Rafe, studying the man who could kill with his bare hands. Logan didn't know if her exhaustion—or intimidation—kept her silent. Holding Lanie carefully, Logan backed into the screen door and held it open while Rafe and Kat walked through.

"The kitchen's through there." Logan tilted his head toward an oak-trimmed entrance. "We'll be upstairs."

"Second door on the left," Rafe added.

The little angel stirred in his arms then snuggled down against Logan's neck. His heart swelled at the trust. He followed Rafe up the stairs and into a bedroom near Logan's own room. Two miniature beds rested side by side, and a large stack of toys piled in the corner. Someone had even remembered diapers and baby powder.

He frowned. "They had cribs in Kat's house. Is a bed safe?"

"*Your* son does gymnastics on his crib. Not only that, he climbed out, then pulled a gun on you before you knew what was happening. A kid like that deserves a bed."

"Yeah, but the trick will be to keep him in it." Logan settled Lanie under a frilly pink comforter. "He's a hellion. Thinks he's invincible."

"Can't imagine who he takes after…." Rafe said, tucking Hayden beneath a comforter covered in fire engines. "There's more stuff downstairs. Zane's sister has kids. She told us what to get."

"Thanks." Logan stared down at his children. He couldn't take his eyes off them.

Rafe put his hand on Logan's shoulder. "You're a lucky man."

He cleared his throat. "Yeah."

"We won't let anything happen to them."

"It's not going to be easy," Logan said, easing quietly into the hallway. "What have you found out about the people coming after us?"

"We have at least two distinct players, maybe more."

"Agreed. The king wants a live heir, but whoever tried to burn down the barn wants Kat dead. What about the guy I killed at the hospital?"

"Zane got hold of the morgue photos. He came up with an ID. It took some digging, but bottom line, the man's associated with Victor Karofsky."

Logan stilled in recognition. "Karofsky. Three years ago."

"You cost him millions when you took down the Uzbekistan arm of his operation."

"His son ran things. He was killed."

"You almost died," Rafe said. "You had no choice."

"Is Victor after my family?" Logan whispered. "Does he want Kat dead?"

"It fits. The blood from the guy you shot at the barn matches evidence at the babysitter's murder scene. We don't have a name. Whoever he is, he likes knives and has used them before. Just Victor's type. One slice across the throat."

"Dammit, I gave her money and told her to get out of there. Why didn't she run?"

"Your envelope was still in her purse, but get this.

Several thousand dollars were direct deposited into her account yesterday, a few hours before she was killed."

Logan cursed. "Someone must have paid Paulina to put the transmitter in Hayden's fire engine. No one else had the opportunity."

"No. That just can't be true." Kat's harsh whisper erupted. "It can't."

Logan spun around.

Kat stood at the top of the stairs, her gaze pained. "Paulina wouldn't betray us like that."

Logan strode down the hallway toward Kat and she met him partway. "I'm sorry, but there's no doubt her killer was the shooter from the ranch. Nothing else fits."

Kat swayed as the truth of the betrayal hit, and Logan slid an arm around her. She leaned into him.

"Tell Zane to get me a visual on whoever deposited that money into Paulina's account," Logan ordered Rafe. "If he can't, get a financial forensic expert to track the money back."

"Got it."

"I want the tactical team in the situation room at dawn, with Hunter on video conference. We'll be bringing in more men to guard here. Also, find out if Noah Bradford is still in Europe. We may need to tap him for information on Victor's latest dealings with terrorist organizations."

"Terrorists?" Kat blanched. "We have terrorists after us?"

"My cue to leave." Rafe disappeared down the hall.

Kat searched Logan's face. "I don't understand."

"I'm making some assumptions," he said. "We'll know more soon. In the meantime, the kids are asleep and safe." He drew Kat against his chest, holding her tightly to him.

"I need to see them."

Logan nodded, then eased open their door showing her the room Rafe and his men had created. A small night-light glowed, illuminating the twins, who were sound asleep, cuddled beneath the covers.

She looked around. "You did this for them?" She gazed up into Logan's eyes, stunned. "How?"

"It's one of the perks of not going it alone. Others help you. Get used to it. You're not struggling by yourself anymore."

Tears filled her eyes, surprising Logan, but he was even more shocked when she rose on her tiptoes and kissed him on the cheek.

"Thank you."

Exhaustion laced her eyes, but something else shone there. Uncertainty. Yearning? It struck him that for the first time, he and Kat were standing together, as parents, watching their children sleep under his roof. Something shifted deep inside him, breaking down defenses he'd thought unassailable. A protectiveness surged, stronger than he'd ever felt. He wanted her with him. He didn't want her to leave. The sting at the back of his eyes stunned him.

"Logan?"

He didn't say a word, just led Kat into his bedroom. She hesitated in the doorway.

"Stay with me tonight."

She glanced around nervously. Her gaze locked on the baby monitor beside the bed. She bit her lip.

"They're right down the hall," he said softly. "We won't do anything but sleep. Just stay. Let me hold you and protect you."

Fatigue must have weighed her down, because her shoulders sagged and she nodded.

The next minute she was in his arms.

He kicked the door shut and latched it, then stood, simply cradling her against him.

"I'm afraid, Logan, and I don't want to be."

Her soft curves fit against him, evoking oh-so-sweet memories of beach breezes, waves breaking outside their door and endless days of passion. His body hardened in response as her familiar floral scent encircled him, but he'd promised.

He cupped her cheek and her ice-blue eyes stared up at him. "Shhh, everything's going to be all right."

"I want to believe that."

He did, too. He'd make it be all right...somehow.

He pulled her to the bed, but just sat on the side, not expecting anything more.

She joined him and ran her hand over the dark suede coverlet on his king-size bed. "I didn't think I'd ever be here," she said, her voice sounding almost awestruck.

He took her hand and twined their fingers. "I imagined it more times than you know."

Logan's heart raced at the flaring passion in her eyes. A look he knew all too well.

"What's going to become of us, Logan? Everything seems against a happy ending. Can I really just walk away from the king?"

"I have a few suspicions about King Leopold's dealings that I doubt he would want made public. I could use the information to 'reason' with him. *If* that's what you really want."

"I don't want to be in his life."

"Think hard, Kat." Logan couldn't believe he was saying this. "Leopold is family."

Her body stiffened. "That man is *not* my father. He

was a sperm donor. He left my mother struggling to fend for us."

She froze at the flinch crossing Logan's face. Kat could tell hurt rode hard on his shoulders.

"Kind of like me."

Kat gasped. "No. Nothing like you! You cared about the kids as soon as you knew they existed. The king never cared enough about my mother and me to even check on us."

"He didn't find out about you until your mom died."

"Almost four years ago!" Her eyes flashed again. "He's known for all that time and he didn't so much as try to find out about me until he decided I might be useful to him."

Logan's hand stilled. The king *had* been interested in her. A little over three years ago, after the king's son Max had been killed, he'd ordered Logan to track her down. That's why he and Kat met. That's why Hayden and Lanie existed.

The unspoken lie rose between them and doused his desire like a plunge in a frozen lake. How would she react to the truth? "Kat—" he began.

She shook her head. "You don't understand. You have a *place* you call home. I don't care about that. All I want is to give my kids a chance at a better life. I don't care where. But it won't be with someone who wants me just because my DNA happens to be half his."

A sharp knock sounded at their door.

"Come."

Rafe cracked open the heavy oak, a frown on his face. "We need you downstairs. Hunter just contacted Noah regarding the terrorists. He's in Bellevaux tracking a rumor. Daniel might still be alive."

THE CEMENT TRUCK SAT in the corner of the construction site. Deke Powell slammed his hand on the steering wheel. He'd tracked the transmitter to its final destination. Damn, Logan Carmichael. This was the second time they'd lost him.

Victor wouldn't be happy. His partner Hans had nearly turned that big knife he carried on *him*.

Deke's cell phone rang. He glanced at the number and felt the blood drain from his face. Victor Karofsky ran his organization without tolerance or mercy.

"Powell." Perspiration beaded on his forehead.

"Are they dead?" The Russian accent never failed to give Deke chills, or perhaps it was the cold efficiency behind the words.

He swallowed. "Not exactly, sir."

Silence reigned over the phone.

His hand shook.

"Your orders were to kill the princess and her children, not to mention Logan Carmichael," Victor spat.

The cold, quiet voice sent a chill of foreboding skittering up Deke's spine. "I will find them." He prayed the vow was true.

"I don't give second chances."

"I know where they are," he lied. "Please. I'll take care of them."

The phone went quiet and a woman's sobs sounded in the background. Deke gripped the phone, terror icing his veins. No, it couldn't be his wife....

"Deke?"

Oh, God. "Maria?"

"Please, Deke. Help me."

Maria screamed, the sound horrifying.

"I said I'll kill them," he yelled. "Leave her alone!"

"Yes, you *will* kill them," his boss spat into the phone. "I won't tolerate another failure from you."

A loud thud sounded through the phone. His wife howled in agony.

Maria!

"I think you are beginning to understand me."

"What did you do?"

"Let's just say that I'll keep her wedding ring finger on ice for you. Fail me again, Powell, and that's all you'll ever have of her."

KAT AWOKE TO RAYS OF WINTRY dawn shining on her face through the slats in the window. Two sets of giggles erupted and she flipped to her side to face the children. Their blue and hazel eyes were alight with laughter as they peered over the edge of the mattress.

"Big bed," Lanie said, her hazel eyes blinking. "Up, Mommy."

Kat picked up Lanie and Hayden and they crawled all over Logan's huge king. He hadn't come back last night. She'd finally dozed off waiting for him, but the other side of the bed remained made. Someone had covered her with a blanket, though.

Hayden threw himself on top of her and giggled. She hid her concerns, and spent a precious moment wrestling and laughing with her kids.

They huddled against her until finally Hayden sat up. "Hungry."

"Me, too," Lanie said. She crawled to the edge of the bed and looked down. Her nose wrinkled up and she frowned. "Too high."

Logan swooped into the room and scooped Lanie into his arms. "Hey, I heard someone wants to eat? I make a mean bowl of cereal. Want some, short stuff?"

"Daddy," she chortled and grabbed his nose.

Hayden bounced on the bed and reached his hands to the ceiling. "Daddy."

Kat pushed her hair out of her face. She had to look like a mess. Her clothes had wrinkled from the night, and she could sleep for another week. Logan didn't look much better with his fatigue-laden expression.

"You haven't been to bed, have you?" she said, hugging her arms around her legs, drinking in the sight of him.

"No, but believe me, I thought about it a lot."

She blushed, looking from his heated gaze. Strange. She felt almost comfortable. As if this happened all the time and heaven knew that wasn't the case. Letting herself care too much wasn't smart.

Logan settled one kid in either arm. "Want some breakfast?"

"Love some," she answered honestly.

"Okay, meet you in the kitchen. I'll take the kids with me so you can catch a break."

"If you give me a minute, I'll head down with you."

"Hurry up, Mommy!"

True to her word, a minute later she followed him down the stairs. He cradled their children in secure arms. She'd always been strong, but she struggled carrying just one of the kids these days. They were growing up so fast.

A pang of discomfort hit her. He'd missed all that.

Could she make it up to him? And if she did, would she leave herself vulnerable to the inevitable heartbreak that would follow when things didn't work out?

She slid her hand over the banister, the fine wood smooth, shiny and polished beneath her palm. At the bottom of the stairs, she looked around the empty family room. A huge television was mounted on one wall, and a large stone fireplace filled another. The dark brown leather sectional must have cost the earth. She winced at the thought of what her two-and-a-half-year-olds could do to that piece of furniture. Especially Hayden. If left alone, her miniature tornado could demolish anything in the time it took to turn around.

This house wasn't a baby house. It was all man. Not stuffy. Sturdy and elegant in a masculine way. The expensive furnishings and the detailed architecture intimidated her.

She really didn't fit in here.

Lanie giggled as Logan whispered something in her ear. The kids had never seen anything like this place before. Did *they* belong here, even if she didn't? Logan *was* their father.

Unable to dismiss the unease, she followed behind them through the swinging doors into a large kitchen. Double ovens, double stoves, double everything. The scent of fresh coffee filtered through the air. Her mouth watered. "Where is everyone?"

"Downstairs. Working. I'll give you a tour as soon as I feed the troublesome twosome." He blew a raspberry on Hayden's belly and the boy giggled wildly. With the greatest care he placed the kids on booster seats at the large butcher-block table and kissed their heads.

Kat's throat closed up. For one moment, she could imagine them, a family. She shouldn't let herself hope for anything, but she couldn't help it.

He opened the freezer and rifled through its contents.

A salt-and-pepper-haired pixie appeared out of nowhere, sped into the room and slapped his hand. "Get your nose out of there, Logan Carmichael. Just because you own the place doesn't mean you can take over my kitchen while I'm here."

He jumped back faster than Kat would've thought possible, his expression sheepish.

"Sorry, Gretchen," he said and kissed her cheek. "Kat, this is the woman who runs the Triple C."

"It's about time Logan brought a woman home."

Logan sighed and rested a hand on Hayden's head. "And these, Gretchen, are our children, Hayden and Lanie."

Gretchen gave Logan a scowl before turning to Kat with a wide, welcoming smile. Gretchen knelt at the table between the two. "Well, aren't you two the spitting image of your daddy and grandma, God rest her soul. And what would you two be wanting for breakfast this lovely morning?"

Logan's proud gaze flickered with pain at Gretchen's words. He knelt beside Lanie and caressed her hair lightly. "Lanie does have Mom's smile, doesn't she?"

"Aye, the spitting image, my boy."

Gretchen tapped Hayden's cheek. "And I bet this sturdy little boy shovels down food like his daddy did."

"I hungry," Hayden said, wriggling in his chair.

Gretchen laughed. "What do you like to eat, my darlings? Anything you want?"

Lanie's and Hayden's eyes grew big. "C…Cereal?"

Kat winced at their tentative words. So cautious, mostly because Kat had to be so careful with her meager finances. There weren't a lot of extras in their house. Usually there wasn't a choice for any meal.

"Not waffles? Or Pancakes? Or eggs?"

"Pancakes?" Lanie repeated softly. "I like pancakes a whole bunch."

Hayden's eyes lit up. "Mommy! Pancakes!"

Kat frowned at the realization the meal was such a treat. The memory of her own wish for more when she was a child flooded through her. Had she failed her kids on that level, too? She bit her lip then forced herself to smile.

"Sounds yummy, huh, kids?" she choked, looking away, avoiding Logan's questioning glance.

"Pancakes it shall be, dear ones," Gretchen said and placed a huge iron skillet on the burner. "Juice first. Apple or orange?"

"Apple!" they yelled together.

"You got them for a moment, Gretchen?" Logan asked.

The housekeeper nodded, and Logan clasped Kat's hand and drew her into the luxurious living room. He tilted her chin up. "I can see those wheels turning a mile a minute. What's the matter?"

She shrugged, feeling awkward. "I haven't done right by them. They shouldn't be so excited about pancakes for breakfast."

"Stop it. They're great kids, Kat. You're a great mom. They know they're loved and that's most important."

"I work too much. I don't see them enough. I can't give them what they need." She turned away from him and swept her arm in a flourish at the living room. "Look at this place, Logan. I'll never have anything that comes close to what you have."

She bowed her head, and her shoulders sagged.

"What do you see, Kat?"

"That money makes a lot of things possible," she said sadly. "That my whole house could fit in your living room, and, right or wrong, knowing that makes me uncomfortable. That I haven't provided for my kids as well as I'd thought."

Logan shook his head. "Come with me."

He took her through the mudroom and unlatched an

old, weather-beaten wooden door. He ducked his head and led her inside the tiny space. A small rough-hewn bed took up much of the floor space, and an old rocking chair sat in the corner.

"This was the original ranch house. My great-grandfather built it. There's an even older homestead on the backside of the property. My mother told me her great-grandpa wanted to be closer to the creek. There's no water there now, of course, only a dry gully. The point is, when my ancestors started this ranch, they didn't have much."

Kat scanned the walls and stared at a photo of a woman and boy. A boy with hazel eyes. He looked a lot like Hayden except for the hair color.

"That's you."

"With my mom. The ranch has been in her family for five generations." Logan paused. "She left when I was thirteen. The only thing my dad found was a note promising she'd be back. I found a slightly different version. Her intentions weren't so clear. Either way, I guess she decided we weren't worth it, because we never heard from her again."

Kat didn't know what to say.

"This house may possess the facade of wealth, but be careful what you assume about me and my life. Your little house was full of love. I left home at eighteen before my dad beat me to death."

"No." She pictured a young man in constant fear of his life. How had Logan become the strong man standing before her? How had he overcome his past?

"Believe me, Kat, if there's no love in a house, the rest is just trappings."

He brushed past her, but she stopped him with her arm. "Logan, I'm sorry about your mom."

He stopped and heaved out a sigh. "Yeah, me, too."

"Why did you ever come back?"

"To save the ranch. I belong to the land," Logan said simply. "That's my legacy. My grandmother would have wanted me to save it. She loved it. Everything I did was for her. *She* loved *me,* and that's not something I take lightly."

Kat didn't know what to say. She'd assumed so much about him, and she'd been so wrong. She wanted to walk into his arms. He'd been left alone, in more ways than one. At least her mom had stayed.

Why couldn't she reach out to him? What was stopping her?

She was a fool.

Logan walked back toward the kitchen. Alone.

Kat just couldn't follow.

THE CHILL IN THE WINTER AIR didn't faze Logan, but he'd never seen anything in all his years that prepared him for the way his kids had wrapped his employees around their proverbial little fingers. He'd been undercover with these men, faced death alongside them, and here they were entertaining his two children like rodeo clowns.

Hayden ran fearlessly around them, laughing, unaware that terrorists in some parts of the world trembled when they simply heard these men's names.

Lanie sat on the steps, petting a tabby kitten, joy lighting her blue eyes as the tiny furball crawled all over her. He wondered which barn cat had had kittens and where she'd hid them this time. From the looks of it, Lanie intended this ranch kitty to become a house cat. Wouldn't Gretchen be thrilled?

Logan sent Kat a sidelong glance. He couldn't figure her out. She seemed drawn to him, and yet so cautious.

He didn't doubt what a good mother she was, though. She watched over her children, always vigilant and protective.

Lanie stumbled in the dirt, chasing the kitten, and Kat leaned forward, ready to grab her, but Tim, his newest ranch hand, swept Logan's daughter up off the ground and dusted her off.

Lanie gave Tim an air kiss, hugged his leg and looked over at Kat. "Mommy, I falled down!" Her lip quivered.

"Yes, sweetie, but you're fine. Mr. Tim saved you."

Lanie gifted the young man with a brilliant smile then went back to playing with the kitten. From the besotted expression on the poor guy's face, he'd lost his heart to the little charmer.

Logan moved closer to Kat. Her freshly washed hair and skin smelled of lavender and verbena. Her makeup-free skin begged for his caress. Man, she was beautiful.

"They're amazing."

"You have to watch them every second, though."

"I don't think that'll be a problem," Logan said as Hayden stumbled. His foreman steadied the boy.

"Tim, get back to Prancer. Mr. Willis will be sending the carrier soon," the foreman ordered.

Kat turned in surprise. "You have dealings with Rance Willis?"

The man was a legend around Carder. He'd appeared out of nowhere and taken over a huge section of land. Within a few years, his quarter horses were winning futurities all over the region. Her old boss, Mr. Daughtery, had been trying to get him to buy stock since he'd arrived.

"Rance is a…colleague," Logan said. "I have a few customers who pay for Prancer's stud services."

"I thought this was a cattle ranch?"

"It used to be a profitable one," Logan said, in frustration. "My father ran off the customers, drinking away the profits until he buried himself in debt. By the time I came back, there was no way to salvage the operation. I had to sell the stock just to hang on to the place."

"How do you survive?"

"A bit of horse breeding, and my investigative and security work."

She arched a brow. "I thought most investigators worked out of a bad neighborhood and barely made ends meet."

"I deal in international security," Logan said. "My interests are more…complex than your standard P.I."

"You mean dangerous," Kat said. "How did you come to work for the king?"

"I met him through your half brother, Prince Stefan," Logan said quietly.

Kat's eyes dimmed. "You knew my brother?"

"Yeah." Logan thought of the last time he'd seen Stefan. Across the ballroom. Minutes before the bomb blew the royal court to smithereens.

The scar on his cheek burned, a reminder of how he'd fought to find Stefan, but hadn't been able to find him in the burning wreckage. The only reason he and Leopold were alive was they'd stepped out into the hallway for yet another argument seconds before the blast.

Forensic teams were still trying to identify the bodies from the area where Stefan had been. What a tragic waste.

A loud whinny sounded from a barn and Tim raced out of the red building into the attached paddock, followed by a very angry horse.

Tim vaulted over the fence and Prancer rose and batted the air with his hooves.

"Tim!" the foreman yelled. "What the hell is going on?"

The man came to a halt and let out a sigh. "Apparently Prancer isn't in the mood to donate and ensure his future bloodline."

"Amateur," the foreman muttered. "Lucky the damn horse didn't get hurt."

Tim bowed his head.

Hayden put his fists on his hips and glared at the foremen. "You said a bad word. You're not s'posta do that."

Logan snorted. "You tell him, Hayden."

"Great. Even the boss's kid is a boss." The foreman strode into the pen, but the stallion backed away, rising up. Within a few minutes, it was clear the man was getting nowhere with the riled horse.

Before Logan could say a word, Kat strode across the dirt and straight to the pen. He followed, but didn't stop her when she shoved through the gate.

"Let me try."

The man hesitated to give up his ground. "He's an awful big horse for a little girl like you."

She gave the foreman a sharp look, and he met Logan's gaze in supplication.

"Let her do it," Logan said. Heck, he would've given Kat her way in a heartbeat if she'd given him that kind of glare.

The foreman picked up his Stetson, dusted it off and set it back on his head. "He's all yours. Don't say I didn't warn you."

Kat eased toward the wild-eyed stallion. At first, he paced back and forth nervously, bolting once when she got too near. But slowly, her voice falling to a whisper, she gentled the animal.

The horse's flanks quivered as she came closer.

"Easy boy. Everything is going to be just fine. They

were just trying to rush things a little, weren't they." She held out her hand and moved within a few feet.

The horse's ears twitched, but he stayed still as Kat closed the distance between them. "That's right. You don't have to be afraid of me. I'll take care of you."

Prancer flicked his head, then nudged her with his nose and she rubbed the velvety softness.

"Yeah, those men don't know how to take care of a big boy like you, do they?" she murmured, her hand slipping to his back. "No appreciation for the subtleties, hmm, you handsome animal?"

The horse snorted and Logan grinned as his foreman's mouth dropped open. Kat had the horse practically purring in a matter of seconds.

"Me, too, Mommy!" Hayden called out. "I do it!"

Logan's gaze whipped to his son. Everyone had been so focused on the out-of-control horse they'd lost sight of Hayden. He'd toddled too close to the bull pen.

The Triple C's prized breeding bull, Sweetness, his red eyes narrowed, stared at Hayden. The bull was over twenty-five hundred pounds of mean. The animal snorted and pawed at the dirt.

Logan's heart sank into his belly.

He raced toward his son.

Hayden just smiled up at the bull and stepped closer. "Hi, han'som manimal."

Chapter Five

Logan scooped Hayden up in one arm and darted safely away from the bull. Logan's knees shook as he carried the boy to the steps, sat him down and knelt in front of him. "Don't..." Logan started, his heart still pounding wildly. "Don't ever do that again. You never go near the animals like that, son. Do you understand?"

Hayden stuck out his lower lip. "Mommy did."

"Mommy has training. And she's an adult."

Kat came and stood by Logan's side, visibly shaking as she confronted Hayden. "What did we tell you when we came out here? Stay with a grown-up. Time out. Now."

Hayden crossed his little arms in front of him. "Lanie's not with a gwown-up. She's with a kitty."

Logan looked around, searching for his daughter. "Where *is* Lanie?" His heart stuttered. He scanned the pens, the outside of the barn, the yard. No pink coat. His little girl was nowhere in sight.

"Logan, I don't see her. She was here a second ago!"

"Find Lanie!" he shouted to his men, who split off to look.

"Logan, where would she go?" Kat cried. "Where's the kitten?"

Gretchen came out on the porch. "What's going on?"

"Lanie is missing." Kat carried Hayden up the stairs. "Gretchen, please take him in the house and put him under lock and key while we look for Lanie."

Gretchen took Hayden and turned toward the door.

"Gretchen, wait!" Logan shouted. "Do you know where the orange barn cat had her litter? Lanie was playing with one of the kittens a few minutes ago."

Fear crossed the housekeeper's face and she glanced over at the construction zone, with its huge piles of broken wood and old, rusty nails. "She always had her litters in the barn you tore down."

Cursing, Logan headed for the yellow construction tape. He'd recently had the oldest barn on the property torn down and there was still debris everywhere. During their tour of the ranch, this had been the one area Logan had absolutely forbidden the kids to go.

Except the stacks of lumber would be a perfect place for a mother cat to hide her kittens.

Lanie had behaved so much more passively than her brother, Logan had been more afraid that Hayden would cross the barrier.

One by one, his hands came out from inside and behind buildings shaking their heads. This was a nightmare. How had he ever thought he could be a good father? He couldn't even keep track of two little kids. If anything happened...

Logan cupped his hands. "Lanie!"

Kat joined him, calling her daughter's name.

"Mommmmmy," a little girl's voice cried faintly.

Logan spun around. "Wait! I heard something!"

The sound had come from behind the construction tape.

"Lanie!" he called again. He ducked under the tape and stomped through the rubble. "Where are you, baby?"

"Logan," Kat shouted, heading toward the farthest corner. "I think she's that way."

He twisted back around a stack of corrugated roofing tin in the direction she pointed. The other ranch hands followed him into the area and spread out, periodically calling his daughter's name.

He headed for the biggest pile and peered under the debris, desperation rising in the back of his throat. He had to find her.

"Daaddddyyyy…" Her tiny wail echoed eerily. "I fall down. I stuck!"

"She's nearby. Search for a hole!" he called out to his hands.

Rafe and Zane, his computer expert, appeared by his side. "Gretchen called us. What's happening?"

"Lanie's disappeared out here somewhere," Logan said, his voice gritty and determined.

"We'll find her." Rafe stood by his side.

"Lanie, keep calling out, honey," Kat called.

His baby girl whimpered. "I hurt, Daddy. Mommmmmmy. Help me."

Every cry shredded Logan's soul. He'd seen men die—his men. He'd regretted every lost life, but nothing had prepared him for his child being hurt and afraid.

"I falling!" She screamed louder.

He and Kat raced past the old barn's foundation toward the pasture. Surely she hadn't gone this far. "Yell, Lanie," he shouted. "Daddy will find you."

The men had quieted, straining to listen.

There was no sound.

Chills prickled down Logan's back.

"Lanie!"

He turned back and looked at Kat, the desperation in her eyes nearly crippling him.

He scanned the area. Where could she be? There was one last dump site. The hairs on the back of his neck tingled. He didn't ignore his instincts. Ever. He shoved at another of the twisted remains of the barn's metal roof and reeled back in horror at a pile of rubble.

The old stone well.

No telling how deep.

The planking had broken through.

"Lanie?" He cleared some boards and peered into the dark depths. He gasped. Lanie rested on a thin ledge of earth and rock, blood trickling down her cheek. Unmoving. Her eyes closed.

"I found her! Get Doc."

Logan reached in, but his little girl was too far away. Kat hovered beside him, choking back sobs.

His men raced over, Logan cursed as more stones and debris shook loose inside the well. Logan studied the precarious situation. The earth movers had made the entire area around the well unstable. He had to get her out of there fast. "I need a rope."

Rafe stopped behind him. "You going in?"

"Yeah, the ledge is crumbling."

A ranch hand ran up, bearing a rope. Logan wrapped part of it around his waist, then leaned into the well. "Hang on to this in case the well collapses."

The men grabbed the rope and Rafe guided Logan down. He eased the five feet to where his daughter lay. Dirt sifted alongside of him.

"Get her now, Logan," Rafe said. "It's starting to cave."

One hand gripping her coat, Logan swiftly checked her arms and legs. She didn't look hurt, but there was no real oxygen down there. Her face was freezing, her lips tinged blue. He got a grip under her arms and pulled her to him.

"Get us out of here," he called.

As the men tugged Logan and Lanie toward the top, she blinked her eyes and those baby blues opened to him. She looked startled, then sniffed. "I'm c-cold."

"I know, baby. We're going inside by the fire. Right now."

She nodded and reached her arms around his neck.

Within seconds, the men helped them out.

"Lanie!" Kat cried, running, hugging her child. Tears stained both of their cheeks. "Baby girl, don't scare Mommy again like that. Please."

Logan drew Kat in close and the three of them just stood together for a minute. "Doc will check her out. I think we've all had enough fun for one day."

As he carried Lanie toward the house, Logan started to shake. His first morning on the job as a father and both kids had nearly died. He had a lot to learn about toddlers. They weren't even three and they'd already locked on to danger like heat-seeking missiles. He couldn't wait for their teenage years.

THE FIRE ROARED in the fireplace, and the chill finally left Kat's hands. The ranch hands had gone back outside after hovering over Lanie while Doc checked her out and declared her bruised but okay.

Rafe and Zane had disappeared down the stairs. The family was alone. Sort of.

Kat settled in the leather sofa, spreading a soft blanket over her and her daughter. "You okay, sweetie?"

"I want Cinderella Band-Aids. They gots the wrong kind."

"We don't have any here, honey."

Lanie frowned, looking like a tantrum might ensue.

Hayden came over to his sister. "You got lots of owies."

The admiration in his voice seemed to perk Lanie up.

Logan poured two fingers of whiskey and gave Kat a questioning glance. She shook her head. She didn't need anything else to make her feel like a rotten mother but was sorely tempted after the morning.

Gretchen came in bearing a tray with milk and chocolate chip cookies. "Who wants a treat?"

The cavalry, thank goodness. The question distracted Lanie and she pushed off the couch as Gretchen placed the cookies on the large coffee table.

"That produced a quick recovery," Kat said to Gretchen as the kids leaned over the tray.

"Never underestimate the curative powers of chocolate chip cookies."

Hayden's hand hovered over the cookie and he gave his mother a pleading glance. "Please, Mommy."

"Have you been a good boy today?"

His head dropped and he shook it. "No. I'm naughty."

Kat couldn't help but smile. If nothing else, her son told the truth.

"Are you sorry for not minding me and Daddy?"

He nodded and turned to her. "I sorry, Mommy."

She smiled. "Then I think one cookie is okay."

Hayden grinned and threw himself into her arms and gave her a big kiss before bouncing back to the table. "You get two cookies, Lanie. Cause you have owies."

He gave his sister two cookies. "Here's the big ones."

Kat blinked back her tears. What had she done to deserve them?

Seeing them safe, Kat finally relaxed, weariness settling deep into her bones. Post-adrenaline crash. She rubbed her aching forehead. She didn't know how much longer she could keep it together.

As if he could read her mind, Logan placed his untouched drink on the mantel.

"Is the door locked, Gretchen?"

"Dead bolted," she said meaningfully. "All of them."

"Great. Could you watch the kids for a few minutes?"

"Like a hawk," she said, kneeling next to the coffee table. "I'm on to these two now." She gathered a tote bag from nearby and pulled out crayons, coloring books and several animated movies. "Go on. I've got it covered." She winked. "I'll handcuff them to the cookie tray if I get desperate."

Logan took Kat's hand and led her into the hallway. He pulled her into his arms. She sank into the hard planes of his body and hugged him around the waist. She shivered. "That was too close."

He kissed her hair. "How did you do it alone?" he asked.

"I didn't have wells and bulls in the backyard," she said quietly, "though they find ways to endanger themselves wherever they go. Usually, it's just Hayden, though."

"Baby-proofing takes on a whole new meaning after this morning," Logan said, guilt obviously weighing heavily on him.

The slam of a door pulled them apart. Rafe crossed the foyer. "One of the sensors at the edge of the property went off," he said. "Zane's tracking the video feedback now, plus double-checking the rest of the perimeter."

"What happened?"

"The camera just went dark."

"Take a couple of men and find out what's going on,"

Logan said. "With all the people hunting us, we need to make sure we haven't been compromised. Find out."

Kat's entire body froze in fear. She'd felt safe from the assassins here. What if they weren't safe anywhere?

Logan took her hand. "Come on." He turned to the living room. "Gretchen, we're taking the kids downstairs. Now."

Gretchen's smile vanished and she grabbed the cookies, crayons and movies. "Come along, munchkins. We're going to a special place. It will be fun."

Logan led them all down the stairs into the lowest level of his home and through a heavy steel door. They crossed a large conference room, with a wall of computer monitors and television screens, phones and gadgets straight from a spy movie. Zane sat at a station, his fingers flying over a keyboard.

From his hulking size, Kat would have expected to see him lifting weights all day, not holding reign over a dozen computer screens with sets of data she couldn't identify.

"Find anything?" Logan asked, his voice tense and serious.

"Other than that sensor, the rest are all clear," Zane said. "I'm checking the property, but haven't seen any sign of intruders."

"I'm taking them in until we know," Logan said. "Is Kat set up to access the room?"

Zane pounded a few more keys. "She can now. You're good to go. Just do the final match at the scanner unit."

"Scanner unit?" she asked.

"You'll see." Logan led her to the other side of the room.

The lights and sounds mesmerized the kids, but she

and Gretchen shooed them toward the back wall where Logan stopped.

"Give me your hand."

A wooden mantel encircled the room, and Logan guided her to search beneath the section in front of them. His warm hand cupped hers and he shifted their fingers until she felt a small button.

"Press it," he said. "We've entered your index fingerprint into the system so you have access to the room behind here."

A panic room? Was that what he was talking about? She shifted her finger and pressed the button. A whirr sounded as the paneling in front of them slid open, revealing a large room, half living quarters, half storage.

Hayden ran inside ahead of Gretchen and bounced on the bed in the corner. Kat followed him, peering around.

"There's another communication center here," Logan said, opening a second door. "A computer, phone and a screen showing the area in front of the ranch house. It's reinforced concrete, and has its own back-up generator. Unless your fingerprint is in the system, you can't get in or out."

"Was this a bomb shelter?"

"Originally it was a food storage cellar and a tornado shelter," Logan said. "I just upped the security a bit." He turned Kat in his arms. "If you're ever scared, come here. You can call me from there," he said, indicating a phone surrounded by high-tech equipment. "You don't have to worry about anyone being able to break in."

She bit her lip, looked at the kids and Gretchen having a makeshift picnic on the bed, and sighed. "We're safe here," she said, softly.

Logan's phone rang and he slid it from the case on his belt. Kat moved in to listen.

"What do you see, Rafe?"

"A teenager ran his muscle car off the road," Rafe said. "Crashed through the fence and slammed into the tree. He must have been going pretty fast. The whole thing came down and destroyed his car—and the camera."

Kat sagged against Logan. *A false alarm.*

"Is the kid okay?" Logan asked.

"He'll live, but he's hurt. Doc stabilized him, and we're taking him to the hospital. It'll be faster than calling an ambulance. The hospital knows and the E.R. is on standby. I'll be back soon," his right-hand man said.

"Okay. Make sure there are extra patrols out there."

"Already done, and some men are fixing the fence and clearing the tree off the road. Blake's on his way."

"Copy that." Logan ended the call and walked back to his security man. "You heard?"

Zane's hands were flying over the keyboard. "Everyone's been alerted. The sheriff should be just about there."

"Is everything else still clear?"

"So far as I can tell."

Logan hesitated. Should they stay in the panic room longer? The kids were fussing, and Kat looked exhausted. "Keep me posted," he said to Zane before walking over to the group on the bed. "I guess we're not playing down here, after all."

The two kids protested.

"How about some lunch?" he asked. "Grilled cheese sandwiches?"

"And more cookies?" Lanie jumped off the bed and headed to the stairs.

"Maybe tonight," Kat said with a frown. "You don't

need a sugar rush before a nap. You two have caused enough trouble for one morning."

Gretchen carted the kids up the stairs. Logan shut the door to Zane's command station, waited until the alarm system reset and started after them.

Kat clutched Logan's arm, and they stopped on the stairway. She leaned into him, and let his hand caress her back, feeding off his strength.

"I can't live in fear anymore, Logan," Kat insisted. "Call the king. If this is what my life is going to be like as a princess—constant fear of assassins showing up or royal guards coming after me—I don't want to be one."

"You're sure?" Logan tilted her chin up to meet his. "Most people would jump at the chance to be royalty, even with the inherent danger."

Kat met his gaze sadly. "Not me. I never bought into the princess fantasy, even when I was a kid. I wanted a horse to ride, my mom healthy and at home to tuck me in at night. Other than that, I just prayed not to go to bed hungry," Kat said. "I never expected much more."

"And now?"

"I want to stay alive. I want the life I was building back. I want my kids safe, and I want them to grow up like normal children. I may not be able to provide for them like the king, but things will get better for us. Someday."

Logan stepped away from her, his expression wary. "Do I have a place in your plans, Kat?"

Kat stared down at her feet and shifted back and forth. "I don't know," she whispered. "I never dared include you in my dreams. You were everything I believed I couldn't have."

A flicker of desire sparked in his hazel eyes, the green deepening with his changing emotions. Kat tensed as he stepped closer, but her breath also caught at the way her body reacted to him, as if preparing for his nearness. How could he have this effect on her?

"And if you *could* have me?" he asked, his voice husky. "Would you want me?"

Kat swayed toward him, barely able to stop herself from going into his arms. "I'm still afraid." She hesitated. "We've gone through hell together since yesterday. I've depended on you totally, but we really only had one week to learn about each other, and it's been turmoil since you came back."

"Does that matter? We have two children together."

"We don't know each other very well. What if I'm not what you think?" she whispered softly. "What if it turns out you don't want me?"

"I know a lot about you, Kat." Logan tucked an errant strand of hair behind her ear and Kat took in a shuddering breath. "You're passionate, loyal and you love our children. That's an incredibly attractive—and sexy— combination. I wanted you three years ago. Despite everything, I've never stopped."

He lowered his mouth, skirting her lips, teasing her. Her eyelids fluttered closed.

"Tell me we have a chance," he whispered.

He tugged her closer, and she let him press her body against his, reveling in his strength.

She licked her lips nervously and he groaned. "Do we? Because I will…"

"Logan—" she put a finger to his lips "—shut up and kiss me…"

His mouth took possession of hers. His arms wrapped around her and pulled her tight to him, her softness crushed against every hard plane of his body. His arousal pressed against her belly and her own body softened in response.

Logic abandoned her. She couldn't think about danger or protecting her heart. She could only feel and remember how incredible they were together. He stole every sense and she didn't care. She'd been so lonely. For him, she realized. A partner to raise her kids, but also…for this. His tongue explored her mouth and she dueled with him, needed to taste him.

Instinct took over. She pressed against him and he groaned, backing her toward the wall. He moaned and arched his hips against her. Her hands explored the hard lines of his chest. Suddenly his foot slipped on the step. He laughed. "We're going to kill ourselves on these stairs. And let's hope there are no secret cameras in this hallway."

Kat buried her head in his chest. "I am so embarrassed. What if Zane caught us?"

"I'm sure he's kissed a few women in his time."

"I was all over you, not even thinking about where we were." She brushed the hair back from her face. "I'm not princess material, that's for sure. I'm not refined or sophisticated, and I doubt public displays of affection on the palace stairways would be allowed."

"You're everything I want. You're mine," Logan said, his voice low and determined. "I'm not letting you go again, Kat. We're in this together, unless you send me away."

"I'll never do that," she said. "If only my father would leave me alone."

Logan kissed her forehead. "We'll put an end to this right now." He took his phone and dialed a number, hesitating over the last digit. "Do you want me to tell him?"

She stared into his eyes. "I'm not a coward. I'll do it."

She had to. She wanted to go back to how her life had been before this nightmare ever began. Well, everything except not having Logan in it.

Logan pressed the last button and lifted the phone to his ear. "Sergei, it's Carmichael. Kat wants to speak to King Leopold."

With a shaking hand she took the phone from Logan, looked at him and pressed speaker. His eyes warmed at the show of trust. She took a deep breath.

"Have you come to your senses, Katherine? I'm on a tight deadline. The plane taking me back to Bellevaux leaves soon."

Kat cleared her throat. "I'm sorry, Your Highness. I don't think me being your heir is a good idea. Have a safe trip."

"You can't be serious," the king sputtered. "This is no time for selfishness. You are a princess. You have responsibilities. Are you a fool?"

"My first responsibility is to my children—and keeping them safe. I don't want the crown. Find someone else."

"There is no one else, you foolish woman."

"Watch yourself, Your *Majesty*." Logan's tone brooked no argument. "You have no right to speak to her that way."

"I am the king and her father. I have every right, and this conversation is private, Mr. Carmichael." The king's frustration peaked. "Katherine, your brothers are dead. You are my last remaining child. If it's not you, then be named Regent and put your son on the throne."

"Hayden isn't even three!" Kat shouted. "Find a more distant relative and adopt him. Change whatever law you need to, but leave me alone. My son is not a pawn."

"This is not over," the king threatened.

"Oh, yes, *Father*. It is."

"Goodbye, Your *Majesty*," Logan said. "And, by the way, if it isn't clear already, I quit."

THE STENCH OF THE underground prison made him smile.

The Duke of Sarbonne held the whip in his hand and stared at the unconscious man on the floor.

"Wake him."

The guard swallowed deeply. "Yes, Your Grace."

A huge wave of satisfaction flowed through the duke. He was so close to having everything he wanted.

The prison guard threw a bucket of water on the prisoner's body. He didn't move.

A loud clang of metal slammed down the stone-lined hallways.

"I want him awake. He has information I need." The duke lifted his shined boot to kick. If water didn't work, pain would.

A small gasp sounded from the doorway behind him. The duke whipped around.

"Y...Your G...Grace," Niko stuttered, his face pale. "A word, if I may?"

The duke stared down his aide, watching him tremble. "What is it?"

"The princess has refused the king's command. She's staying in Texas."

"What?" His roar of fury echoed down the hall.

The man on the floor groaned, as if coming to, but the duke ignored him, grabbing his aide by the throat. "Tell me everything," he hissed.

Niko tried to shrink back, but the duke held him inches away.

"S...someone is trying to kill her. There have been several attempts on her life."

The duke stilled. "Her? Not the children?"

"All of them."

He shoved Niko away in a rage, slashed the man on the floor with his whip, then whirled on the older guard. "Get me the information I want from this prisoner, or you'll take his place."

"Y…yes, Your Grace," the man stammered.

Pushing past Niko, Sarbonne strode out of the prison, up the winding staircase and through the secret passage. His servant's quick steps hurried behind him.

"Leave me," Sarbonne ordered, his grin twisted at the relief on Niko's face. He was too much of a coward to be of much use except catching and carrying, but he also feared for his life too much to betray Sarbonne.

The duke dialed a familiar number. "Someone is double-crossing me," he said as a man answered. "It had best not be you, Victor. I need that princess alive. Here. Get her for me."

"That was not part of our arrangement."

"Well, it is now, if you ever want those mineral rights."

Dead silence filled the phone. "You dare threaten me, Sarbonne?"

"I *dare* anything. It is my destiny to sit on the throne of Bellevaux. If you want a taste of my power once I get there, you'd be wise to not cross me now."

Another pause. "I see. I am glad you clarified our arrangement."

The duke relaxed his furious death grip on the phone at the quiet comment. "I'm glad you understand, Victor. I don't care how you arrange it—or who you have to kill—but have your men find her and bring her to me within forty-eight hours."

"Any other...requests?"

"Yes." The duke smiled. "I want her too terrified to make one wrong move once she gets here."

Chapter Six

Logan's phone rang. Again. He pulled it out of his pocket and scowled at the screen.

Kat's face tensed, and she worried her bottom lip. "The king wasn't happy. Maybe…"

"He threatened you." She didn't need to doubt herself. Logan turned off the power and stalked into the situation room. "Zane, I need you to delve into King Leopold's finances. I want solid proof I can use to keep him out of Kat's life."

His computer expert crossed muscular arms in front of his chest and grinned. "I love taking down royalty," he said, and cracked his knuckles. "Can I bring Sierra Bradford in? She's got Europe wired. Particularly the banking system."

"Sierra?" Logan scratched his neck. "You trust her?"

"Oh, yeah. I thought about suggesting she join the team, but she had a personal matter to deal with in Denver. I was going to mention it when she straightened things out."

"You think she'd agree?"

"She's the best. Worth asking."

"*You're* the best."

"For cybersecurity, yep. I won't deny it, but Sierra's a true genius when it comes to financial tracking. Espe-

cially in the EU and former Soviet Union. She's so in-
tuitive about where these scumbags try to hide money,
she's downright scary."

"Make the call." Logan needed leverage, and Sierra
Bradford had the security clearance to make things happen. He didn't need to tell Zane, but Sierra had been on
Logan's shortlist for a while. The fact that she was his
friend Noah's sister made the situation tricky, though.
Noah lived a very dangerous double life, and Sierra may
not be aware of Noah's extracurricular activities. Working for Logan would change that.

Kat looked between Zane and Logan, her eyes curious. "What's Sierra going to look into? What do you
plan to do to my father?"

"His irregular finances have been on my radar awhile.
He's up to something. I'll use the knowledge any way
I have to."

"Blackmail?"

Logan smiled, the plan coalescing in his mind. "I
prefer to call it...wielding a strong influence over his
future decision making. He backs off you and the kids,
or I'll reveal what I discover."

Zane snorted. "A rose by any other name, buddy."

"What has he done?" Kat asked.

"The last few years, King Leopold has had an unusual inflow of cash from an unknown source," Logan
said. "I was tracking it, but when your brother, Prince
Stefan, was killed, my main link to the information disappeared."

The grief of Stefan's murder hit Logan in a fresh
wave. His friend had valued integrity over everything,
and it had cost him his life. "With the king threatening
you and the children, I have more reason than ever to
identify the source of Leopold's secret funds—especially

if his duplicity resulted in the bomb attack against the royal court and the assassins coming after you."

Kat shuddered. "You think finding out his secrets will make him stop? He's a king."

"Of a country on the brink of extinction. Leopold will do anything in his power to prevent information leading to his downfall from being revealed. We need to convince him it's in his best interest to leave us alone—and alive—while he comes up with another heir."

Kat frowned. "He seems awfully confident in his power, Logan. The truth is, he scares me."

"Information—in the right hands—is more powerful than most people recognize." Logan caressed her cheek with his finger. "Let Zane do his work. We're running out of time and Leopold isn't the only one we have to stop."

LOGAN TOOK KAT'S HAND and they climbed the stairs to the main level where Lanie and Hayden were freshly bathed, sacked out on the floor of the living room, huge pillows tossed everywhere. Gretchen watched them with an eagle eye.

"Cartoons," she whispered. "They're entranced."

Were the kids "entranced" enough that Logan could steal some time away with their mother? He let his gaze rest on Kat, taking in the curve of her cheek, the light hitting her blond hair, the smile on her face as she watched their children. They'd been caught up in a whirlwind of events. They needed some time to settle things between them. Did they have a future? Did the heated looks he occasionally caught from her mean anything, or was the ranch merely a safe haven until she could hightail it out of here? He sure as hell didn't want her to sleep alone in that king-size bed again tonight, but…

"If you could do watch duty for a few minutes, I'm going to put the laundry in," Gretchen said. "I'll be right back."

Kat knelt down on the floor between their kids and tickled them. Both children squealed with delight, then rolled around in a jumble of blankets as they tried to tickle her back. Finally, they both tackled their mother, smothering her with hugs and kisses as she held them close.

Logan's heart warmed at the sight. This house hadn't seen much laughter since his mother had left. Even before then he could remember too many times when he'd barricaded himself in his room with the music blaring so he didn't have to listen to his parents fight.

Watching Kat with Hayden and Lanie, Logan longed to join them, but he hesitated. They seemed so much like a...family. Close and loving. Complete. Would he be welcomed?

Gretchen walked back into the room. Her face was stark white and tears filled her eyes. One fist clutched tight to her chest. "Oh, Logan..."

He raced to the older woman. "What happened?"

Wordlessly, Gretchen opened her hand and held out a scratched, heart-shaped necklace.

Logan couldn't catch his breath. "It can't be..."

With a trembling hand he took the jewelry and weighed it in his palm. So light and so devastating in its implications. His mother had been wearing it when she had walked out on him and his father. He felt like the bull gored him and left him to bleed out slowly where he stood.

"It's your mother's," Gretchen choked out. "I'd know it anywhere."

"Where did you find it?" He forced the hoarse whisper from his throat. He couldn't take his gaze away from the tarnished locket, or the dark spots that flaked off the broken chain. If he wet the chain, would the flakes turn red with blood?

Gretchen swallowed back tears. "In Lanie's jacket. The one she wore today when she fell in the well. I turned her pockets before putting it into the washing machine. The necklace fell out."

His mind whirled with the possibilities, and they ate at his gut. He knew the truth. Holding this necklace meant his mother had never made it off the ranch.

Kat came closer. "Logan?" She peered over his shoulder. "What is that?"

A nightmare. He fought the memories of anger and accusations from that last day. *A blessing. A curse.*

An answer, and the start of a million dark, ugly questions that he didn't want to ask. Dear God, how could it still be here?

"It's my mother's necklace. I gave it to her when I was ten. She wore it every day and swore she'd never take it off." He met Kat's troubled gaze. "As far as I know, she kept that promise." He looked down at the broken chain, knowing the force it would take to wrench the links apart.

Struggling to hold himself together, Logan walked into his office off the living room and unlocked the lower drawer in his desk. He removed an evidence bag, a clean sheet of paper, then donned plastic gloves. How convenient, he thought, to be the kind of man to have a crime kit ready for a possible murder on his own property.

What was wrong with this picture?

Gretchen's sob filtered through the doorway, but he couldn't speak. She recognized what his preparations meant. The possibility of his mother's disappearance being a homicide had been raised more than once. Logan knew it, but he couldn't let his mind go there. For a minute...just a minute, couldn't he be a son who might have lost his mother in a far different way?

He sank into the leather chair behind his desk and flicked the clasp. The heart locket opened. A tuft of black hair and the picture of a toddler grinning made his eyes sting.

He touched the photo and closed his eyes, letting memories swim through him. There had been good times. Particularly when his father left on one of his frequent out-of-town trips. His mother's footsteps had lightened; her laughter had pealed through the house.

Lavender scent wafted over him. He blinked at Kat over his shoulder.

"I see Hayden in you."

Logan paused, a bittersweet recollection breaking through his emotions. "My mother said she hoped I'd have a little boy just like me. She loved me so much, she wanted me to be just as happy as her." He snapped the locket closed.

He clenched the evidence bag in his fist. "Do you know how much I hated her for leaving me?" Logan stood up, and stared at the necklace in his palm. "What if she didn't? What if someone stopped her?"

Gretchen and Kat watched him warily, not answering.

He slipped the necklace into the plastic evidence bag, reaching for control he didn't feel.

Logan strode into the living room, plucked his daughter from the pillow jungle and sat with her on his lap in his big leather recliner.

Lanie's eyes had gone wide with uncertainty.

Great. He was scaring his daughter. He could interrogate terrorists or criminals, but how did he drag information out of a two-and-a-half-year-old?

"Sweetie," Logan said, gentling his voice. "Where did you find this necklace?"

Her eyes brightened. "My neckwess! I found it." Lanie reached for the baggie, then scooped it into her hands to thrust toward Kat. "It's for you, Mommy. I saw it and got it all by myself."

Logan, recognizing the pride in his daughter's face, forced himself to calm down.

Kat gave him a supportive smile. "Thank you, Lanie." Kat retrieved the locket. "Now, where did you find it?"

Lanie's bottom lip trembled slightly. "Where the kitty got lost."

Logan could feel the urgency rise within him. "Can you show me?"

His daughter looked down at her hands. "No."

"Honey, why can't you tell us?" Kat asked.

Lanie frowned, obviously upset. "I'm not s'posta go there. Daddy yelled at me cuz I got stuck in the bad place."

Logan turned his daughter to face him. "Lanie, I'm sorry. I was scared. I couldn't find you and I didn't want you to get hurt." He held up the evidence bag. "Was this in the bad place?"

Lanie nodded. "Where the mommy kitty hides her babies. It was stuck on a pointy rock. I had to try really hard to reach it."

"You don't have to go, honey," Kat said, meeting Logan's gaze. "Gretchen, could you distract our little adventurers while we go outside?"

A few minutes later they had donned coats and picked across the construction site until they reached the hundred-year-old well. Logan's crew had moved some of the old boards back over the opening. Years of grit and dirt had covered the original planks, hiding the presence of the well.

He swallowed hard, then pulled the locket out to stare at it again. "I thought she left."

She touched his hand lightly. "I'm here if you need me."

He wanted to believe her. Logan put the locket away. He'd heard words like that before and trusted them. From her. From his mother. From Daniel. On a mission, the situation was different. Lies were part of the game. He could handle the betrayals. He expected them. But when it was personal...he'd been burned by believing in those "implied promises." He'd been wrong—at least twice. He didn't know what to think anymore.

Logan peered under a large pile of discarded barn boards and beams where the mother cat had hidden her kittens. His mind churning with dark thoughts. He snagged a flashlight from his coat pocket, flicked it on and ran it across the ledge where he'd found Lanie. Dried blood still marred the rock, but the stain was darker now, almost black. A lot like the ones on the sharp rock several inches away from the ledge.

He could picture the worst case in his mind, driving dread straight through him. Lanie could've tumbled all the way down the well. Struck her head. His heart twisted in pain. He could have lost her.

If his mother's necklace had been yanked from her throat when she struck that sharp rock on the way down, then she might be... He shone the light into the recesses, slowly scanning one section at a time. Debris blocked most of the view of the bottom, but finally the beam passed over several areas of white and a few flashes of color.

Logan paused his movement, his heart pounding, and leaned against the stone wall, trying for a closer look. Did he want to find his mother here? Knowing if she'd fallen, she'd been injured and probably calling out for help for days before dying? Or had she looked into someone's eyes…a man who'd sworn to always love her…before he pushed her to her death?

Would Logan ever know?

He gripped the stone wall and stood back. Dirt fluttered down the well, echoing on the way down, the hollow sound mirroring his emotions.

Struggling against a childhood dread, Logan rounded the structure to get a better angle and swept the inside surface again, foot by foot. More dark splatters appeared on jutting rocks, and finally the light pierced a deeply shadowed spot beneath a series of crumbling wooden planks.

He could just make out several distinctive white shapes. Human bones. He shined the light farther revealing a human skull. Logan gasped, even though he'd known what he would find. Below the ledge where Lanie had fallen lay the skeleton of his mother.

The mother who had never left.

LOGAN LOOKED SO ALONE, he hurt Kat's heart. He stood, separate and apart, watching as a crane lowered a member of the forensics team foot by foot into the well to take more photographs. She didn't know how long she'd studied his stiff posture. He hadn't budged since the medical examiner he'd had flown in arrived.

The entire day had taken on a surreal quality. Because there was no way of knowing how the body had ended up in the well, the ME was treating the case as a homicide. The guarded looks the workers threw around were telling. They had their suspicions.

Kat couldn't imagine what Logan was feeling right now. She'd suffered the devastating loss of her mother, but that had been to cancer. Not a possible murder. He'd believed he'd been abandoned the last fifteen years, only to find out he was wrong. The darkness and anguish in his eyes were haunting. Did he blame himself for not finding her before this?

Being around Logan this long, she guessed he would.

Investigators, photographers and various crime units spread over the area. Kat walked across the yard, wanting to comfort him, but she hesitated. In the hours since he'd rushed back to the house, he hadn't said much of anything to anyone, except to get this investigation started. He'd disappeared into his office, and a dozen calls later, his disciplined focus got him everything he wanted. She'd never seen law enforcement act so quickly.

Each passing hour etched deeper lines of strain into his lean cheeks.

Did he know he didn't have to be alone anymore? He was trying to remain strong and in control, when this had to be tearing him apart. If only he'd lean on her, like she leaned on him.

The kids were napping. Gretchen waited inside listening for any stir. She knew who needed her—if he let her in. When she reached his side, his shoulders tensed and his hands fisted, but he didn't move. Not knowing what else to do, she lifted his fist to her lips and kissed it gently. When he relaxed his hand, she threaded her fingers through his. "I want to be with you. Is that okay?"

He frowned and stared down at her hand as if their threaded fingers were something strange and unusual. Yet he didn't step away, just nodded.

After a moment of silence, he said, "They've confirmed it's a woman. Thirties or forties." His voice was matter-of-fact, but the husky edge gave his emotions away. "She's been there a long time."

His grip tightened on Kat's hand, but she didn't mention it. "What are you thinking?"

"You don't want to know."

"I do, Logan. Talk to me."

He turned toward her. "I'm thinking that I suck as a son. If that's my...my mother," Logan gestured toward the well, "she's been a few hundred feet from my front door for fifteen years and I never knew it."

She raised a hand to his injured cheek. "You were a kid when it happened."

"It doesn't matter. *I never looked for her*," he insisted. "I just figured she ran off. I was lying in my bed crying and cursing her for leaving me on my birthday, while she was out here dying." He swore. "What a selfish jerk I was. I probably still am." He shook his head and backed off. "Sorry. Now is not the time for me to be around anyone."

Screaming sirens and red and blue strobe lights from an approaching vehicle stopped Kat from responding. The noise drowned out the sound of the crane. An SUV barreled down the road and skidded to a halt in front of the house.

Two men exited the sheriff's vehicle and walked toward them. Logan greeted them, not even a tinge of emotion in his voice.

Kat stood nearby, wishing she could hold him tight and not let him go.

Logan took in a deep breath and reached out his hand to the sheriff. "Thanks for coming, Blake." Logan nodded at the other man. "Deputy Parris."

Logan gestured her way. "This is Kat. Protective detail."

She stiffened, then turned to look at Logan, stunned. *Protective detail?* In other words, a client? Icy hurt swept through her. It was all she could do not to cry.

The sheriff, a tall, striking man, touched the tip of his Stetson and nodded in acknowledgment, "Ma'am."

Deputy Parris followed suit.

The sheriff, his hazel eyes worried, gazed at the madhouse around them. "Sorry it took us so long. Serious accident on the road out to Big Springs," Blake said. "What's the latest?"

"I think we found my mother's body."

Both the sheriff and his deputy froze in place.

"Your ma never left?" Parris finally blurted out. "But I remember hearing—"

Blake cleared his throat cutting off the deputy's words.

"You can say it," Logan interjected. "Everyone thought she abandoned me and my father. Including us. My father pretty much drank himself to death after that." Logan looked out across the ranch, the only legacy he had left from his mother. "I can't believe she was here all the time."

Blake tilted his Stetson back. "How'd you find her?"

"My daughter was chasing a stray kitten and fell down an old, covered-up well."

"Whoa. Hold on." The sheriff stepped back. "Since when do you have a daughter?"

Kat felt her face flush and the sheriff's gaze flashed from her to Logan, then returned to her, his eyes narrowing this time. Not necessarily in a friendly way.

Logan ignored Blake's question about his daughter

and gave him a factual rundown of Lanie finding the necklace.

"I tore down the old barn to make room for a new building," Logan ended. "Dad had closed off this area about ten years ago. He said these outbuildings and the grounds were too unstable. The earth movers have really churned things up lately."

Kat recognized the speculation in the sheriff's eyes.

"Your father closed this area off?" Blake ventured. "Have you considered—"

"That he killed my mom and hid the body? Hell, yeah."

Kat froze in shock. Logan suspected his father of killing his mother? Her heart ached for him, but her mind worried. The disconnected expression on Logan's face. She barely recognized the man she'd begun to care for again.

"What do you remember from that day?" Blake pulled out his notebook. "Did they fight?"

Logan nodded. "My father was a mean SOB when he got drunk and he'd really tied one on that day. He told her he hated the ranch and everything about it because it was hers. Hated that my mom had more than him and she'd told him straight up, the ranch was mine if she died. If he could've sold it, he probably would have, but she left it in my name and told everyone about it. Instead, he did his best to gamble it away."

Kat couldn't imagine what Logan had gone through growing up. Instinctively, she reached out and clasped his hand. To her surprise, he held it tightly in his grasp.

Blake closed his notebook. "I think we'd better talk some more later."

Logan nodded, but his face showed no emotion now—as if he'd gone back behind his protective wall, but his hand squeezed Kat's and she responded in kind, letting him know she was there for him.

Blake's gaze dropped to their linked hands and he quirked a brow at Logan. "You say your little girl found the necklace? Can I talk to her?"

"The twins are in the house," Logan said. "It's been rough. I interviewed her. She's not really old enough to be much help."

Blake stopped, putting his notebook away in his pocket. "Twins?"

"Boy and girl. Two and a half years old."

"Okayyyy," the sheriff drawled. "I guess I need to come around more often to keep up with the latest events."

Kat could see all the facts Logan had thrown out registering in Blake's mind. She could tell from his expression he knew a lot more about her than she'd originally suspected. She was the woman who had run from Logan three years ago, and now she was back with two kids in tow, obviously in dire financial straits based on her clothing. Did he see her as a gold digger? Is that how all Logan's friends would see her?

Her grip tightened on Logan's hand, but he subtly shook it off as an attractive woman in a coroner's jacket walked toward them. The woman had come to a crime scene dressed in a suit and heels? Was she kidding? She must've been called away from some fancy function.

Kat's old insecurities flared at the woman's put-together appearance compared to her own faded jeans and much-worn shirt. She remembered all too well how everyone had laughed at the hand-me-down clothes that her mother had patched and rehemmed over and over, in the hopes the tattered material would last through another season.

The woman greeted everyone as old friends, her smile teasing and comfortable. Kat could learn to hate her. Or really like her, more's the pity. "Logan. Blake. Deputy Parris." Her glance skimmed over Kat, to whom she gave a quick nod when Logan finally made introductions, with even less information than before.

"Debra," Blake said, "what do you know so far?"

Doctor Sandoval sent a quick, sympathetic look to Logan. "Lots of trauma, but that's to be expected from the depth of the well. We found her purse. Her license was in it. There's little doubt it's Hannah Carmichael." She hesitated. "I'm sorry, Logan. I know how close you two were, but perhaps this will give you a sense of closure that she's been found."

"Did she…" Logan began, his voice so soft they were barely audible. "Was she…beaten?"

Sorrow lit the coroner's eyes. "I can't tell yet."

"I want to know."

"I won't keep anything from you. I remember what you went through." She placed her hand on his arm and met Logan's gaze, a connection between them briefly flaring.

Kat recognized the familiarity, the softness in the woman's eyes. The awareness in their touch. They'd been lovers once. Had Kat's coming here interrupted something? Her stomach roiled. No, Logan would have told her, but it was obvious that Debra Sandoval still had strong feelings for him.

"Dr. Sandoval."

The coroner turned toward one of the workers and nodded at him before facing Logan. "I'll keep you informed, and I promise I'll get you every answer possible." She kissed his cheek. "Again, I'm *so* sorry about your mother."

Dr. Sandoval offered quick goodbyes to the others before following the worker back to the site.

Kat watched Logan's lover go. The woman was beautiful, sophisticated, educated. A doctor. Everything Kat wasn't. Someone who would fit into Logan's life. Suddenly, Kat's place next to him didn't feel quite so comfortable. He hadn't reached for her hand again after he'd let her go. Perhaps Dr. Sandoval had reminded him of what he could have, while all Kat had brought him was trauma.

He'd been so amazing from the moment he'd saved her life, she'd started to take his presence for granted, to assume the feelings sparking between them were real. To him, maybe she *was* just a protection detail.

She couldn't take the uncertainty. "I need to check on the kids," she said, trying to push down the hurt and confusion rising in her throat.

Logan nodded, but barely glanced her way. "I'll send one of the men with you."

No more living in a fantasyland. She might be a princess, and Logan a brave, handsome protector who'd saved both her and her children, but none of that mattered, except in fairy tales.

As the crime scene illustrated all too well, real life didn't always have happy endings.

A SHOUT CAME FROM deep within the well. Debra Sandoval orchestrated her men. She was good at her job. One of the best—which is why Logan had sent for her, even if she was based several hours from Carder.

She'd tell him the unvarnished truth. Childhood friends tended to do that.

Blake slugged his shoulder. "You're an idiot."

Logan turned to his other closest friend. "What'd you do that for?"

Blake nodded back to the house where Kat had disappeared behind the front door. "She's the one you told me about. The one who sent you into that tailspin a few years back. Isn't she?"

"Okay, that subject is closed."

"Fine. Why are you ignoring her? She's gorgeous."

Logan frowned at his friend. "You're married."

"Very happily, I might add, but, if Amanda were here, she'd slug you, too."

"I haven't done anything."

"If this is the way you treat the women you care about, no wonder you're single. You're a fool."

"Certifiable," Deputy Parris added, his gaze narrowed.

Logan didn't get his friends. "What are you talking about?"

"You were staring at Debra. Kat could tell."

Logan scanned the crane, trying to hear what the workers were saying. "I was talking to her. Debra's the coroner."

"Kat thinks you and the good doctor were lovers," Parris blurted out.

"What?" Logan looked back at the house, where Kat hovered at the window, watching. "How could she know—"

He flushed. "Deb and I make better friends. We just should've kept it that way, but, hell, I've known her since I was six. *We're just friends.*"

"Then," said Parris, "I suggest if you care about the woman who was holding your hand—before you shook it off when your 'we-are-just-friends' buddy showed up—that you take some time to explain it to Kat, because that lady looked mighty hurt and upset when she left."

Logan cursed under his breath. "Kat is the mother of my children. No comparison."

"But," Blake interrupted, "you didn't mention that fact when you introduced her to us. Did you?" Blake said. "I believe the romantic term used was *protection detail*."

Parris snorted. "Boy, you're never gonna make it as a Casanova with those lines."

Logan glared at them both. "We haven't exactly worked things out yet."

"The way you're headed, you may be permanently in the doghouse. I suggest you get inside and sweep her off her feet, Logan. You do know how do that, or should I teach you?"

"I seem to remember things weren't all that easy with Amanda there for a while."

"But I got my head out of my butt and told her I loved her. Are you willing to do the same?"

Logan had no pithy answer. *Was he? Did he love Kat?* His emotions were all in a turmoil. He didn't want to make another mistake.

At that moment, a shout drew his attention. A black body bag was lifted out of the well. He wanted to keel over. He walked across the yard and stood beside Debra as the workers slid his mother's body into the back of the coroner's van.

"Do you need a moment," she asked, touching his arm. He stared at her hands and realized that they didn't offer comfort, not like Kat's did. He shook his head. "Just get me an answer."

She nodded and climbed in beside the body.

Logan went numb as he watched the vehicle leave.

How had this happened? The antlike workers continued to process the scene. Logan needed...he needed Kat.

"Watch them for me," he said to Blake, indicating the forensic teams and other workers. "Just, keep things going..."

"I'll be here doing my job, Carmichael. Now go do yours."

Logan crossed the yard and climbed the steps to the house. Kat had disappeared from the window. He entered and Gretchen stood in the doorway, her face creased with a frown. She nodded her head into the living room. "She's that way. Good luck."

"Thanks," he said, hovering at the entrance.

Kat sat on the floor next to the large stone fireplace, arms wrapped around her knees, staring into the flickering flames. She appeared lost in thought, and unbelievably sad. When his boots sounded on the wood floor, she stiffened and didn't turn to face him.

He knelt beside her and touched her shoulder.

She edged slightly away.

"Kat, there's nothing between me and Debra."

"But there was."

"Briefly."

"I could tell. She seems like she'd be perfect for you. A doctor. Smart." Kat glanced at him from beneath her lashes. "She'd fit in here."

He turned her slowly until they were directly across from each other. "She's not a jigsaw puzzle piece and we make better friends than anything else."

Kat pointed to the painting above his fireplace. "That's a famous picture, isn't it?"

Logan nodded.

She exhaled in frustration. "Look, Logan. I'm glad

you know about Hayden and Lanie, but I don't belong here. We have really different backgrounds—"

"Yeah, you're a princess and I'm a rancher whose father murdered his mother."

"Don't be obtuse," she snapped. "When this all gets straightened out with Leopold, we'll work out visitation rights and…and…"

"You'll just go away."

"It's for the best."

She could stab him in the heart without even trying. Logan met her determined gaze. He didn't like the stubborn glint. Not one bit. But more than that, her words stung. Hard. He'd never treated her like less. He'd done everything in his power to show her he cared. He needed her, and she just wanted to throw everything away.

"Honey, I may be obtuse, but I don't think it's for the best. Not for me, anyway." The words echoed in his memory. Had his mother and father had this same conversation? Was history repeating itself? "What if I don't want you to go, Kat? What would you say to that? What if I want you and the kids to stay with me? What if I think your jigsaw piece fits just fine?"

She stared at him, and he could swear hope flared in her eyes.

"You can't mean that," she whispered. "Oh, God, Logan. I can't make a mistake. What if it doesn't work out?"

He went all in, gambling more than his father ever dared. He caressed her arms, trying to loosen the tension vibrating from within her. "Something is growing between us, Kat. Something powerful. We owe it to ourselves to find out where that will go."

She shivered at his touch. "What if chemistry and feelings aren't enough? I can't afford to be wrong about us. If the kids think we're going to be together, and we don't make it, they'll be devastated. I have to consider these things. I'm their mother."

"And I'm their father." Logan stood and faced her. He'd lost his family. He'd lost Kat once, too. He could not bear to lose his children. "This ranch is their legacy. They'll be the sixth generation of Carmichaels raised here. I didn't fight to keep this place for my grandmother and my mother to not have my children enjoy their birthright."

He crossed his arms in front. "So, what'll it be? Fight or flight? Or can we just move on to the kiss and make up part?"

When she hesitated, Logan just shook his head, disappointment souring his throat. "Think about it and decide what you're going to do. I'll be upstairs in my bedroom. Just know that if you really decide to go for this, once you're inside that room, you may not be coming out for a while."

Chapter Seven

Kat couldn't speak. Her entire body froze with uncertainty. He'd asked her for much more than one week forgetting the world outside. He wanted more. Possibly everything.

Logan stared her down, gauging her reaction as the effects of his challenge ricocheted through her. She swallowed but couldn't hold his gaze. Something indefinable crossed his expression. Hurt? Disappointment? Grief?

"If you change your mind, you know where I am. I have some things to check on."

He left her standing alone in the room and climbed the stairs, disappearing from view. Kat took a deep breath. What was she supposed to do? She wrapped her arms around herself and shivered.

"What in heaven's name are you thinking, girl?" Gretchen's voice pierced the large room. "Do you need an engraved invitation?"

Kat whirled around and faced the slight housekeeper, the woman's frown as intimidating as the unknown future. "You were listening?"

Gretchen laughed. "Of course I was listening. I'm the housekeeper. That's part of my job. You don't think this group of testosterone-driven men could handle saving the world without my guidance, do you?" She stepped closer. "Now it's your turn. What's your intention toward my boss? Make it good, because I've helped him get over you once, and it was ugly. I won't have him put through that kind of pain again. His romp with you left him devastated and volunteering for every suicide mission available—and he almost succeeded three years ago in Germany."

"The coma?" Kat asked, shattered that her children could have lost their father before they ever knew him, that she could have lost Logan.

"The very same, so think hard before you walk away from him this time."

Kat frowned. "You don't understand. I'm not trying to hurt him. I'm trying to protect everyone."

"That's horse manure and you know it. You're protecting yourself. You're afraid to accept all of Logan. Who he is—what he was." Gretchen planted her hands on her hips. "Do you think I've been a housekeeper all my life?"

"I don't know."

"Sure you don't," Gretchen said, "but I grew up in a house bigger than this one. My father was rich…and the man I married at twenty-one was wealthy enough to make Logan look like a pauper." Gretchen grabbed a dish towel from the laundry basket she'd set on the chair and started folding. "Do you think less of me because I now keep house for a living?"

"Of course not!" Kat denied. "A lot of people's circumstances change."

"Ah, but mine didn't." Gretchen set the towel down. "I was a pampered girl, and I enjoyed the money and freedom wealth gave me. I could still be living that same privileged life, but after my husband died and my dearest friend disappeared, I chose to be here on this ranch, watching over her son. For damn sure, the boy's drunken father wouldn't take care of him."

Kat stared at Gretchen, seeing her in a new light.

"Life is all about choices. Logan Carmichael is a good man. The best. But because you doubt yourself, you let him walk out of this room with his heart breaking in two."

"His heart isn't broken." Kat choked. "It can't be. We don't know each other well enough."

Gretchen clicked her tongue. "Maybe that's the real problem. You really don't know anything about him, do you?" She gestured around the room. "He pulled this place back from the auction block. It wasn't so great or fancy looking by the time his father nearly destroyed it. Logan Carmichael knows how to go hungry and be afraid in the night, but you won't let yourself see that part of him. You can't see past the trimmings of what is here now."

Shame struck deep, and Kat tried to turn away.

Gretchen cut her off. "Logan is a hero. While you thought he was drinking champagne, he was probably crawling on his belly through hellholes you and I can't even begin to imagine. He's lived and hunted amidst squalor and danger, tracking evil men and stopping them, while the rest of us enjoyed the safety he won at such personal cost. Three years ago, he came within inches of being listed on the CIA's memorial wall. Because he was distracted by a broken heart."

Kat choked back a cry. "It's not possible." Could he care that much?

"You honestly think a man like that gives a rip about where you come from? To him, money is nothing but a means to help make the impossible possible. To make something good happen for others. But deep down, family and this ranch mean everything to him. He left the CIA to come back and save the Triple C because it was his mother's. Even when he was angry at her, he honored her memory." Gretchen whisked another dish towel to fold from the pile. "In caring for her only son, I've done the same. Now that his mother's body has been found, he'll need even more. He needs you."

Kat shrank under Gretchen's tirade. "What if it doesn't work out?" she whispered. "I have to protect my children."

"Then show them you're brave enough to take a chance on a man who'd give up his life for you and your kids."

Kat looked at the stairs, then hesitated.

Gretchen cursed. "You know, maybe you called it right the first time. Maybe you don't merit him. That man deserves to be happy, and if you're too scared to grab the brass ring when it comes up and smacks you in the face, maybe you should just slink out of here when the danger's gone. You'll only have the whole rest of your life to regret it."

Gretchen stalked into the kitchen, not looking back.

Kat stared after her, then up the stairs. Well, that Irish temper made her feel about one inch tall. And the truth of it, Gretchen was right. *She was a coward.*

She'd have to shove these doubts away. She'd fought to get into nursing school. She'd negotiated to change her work schedule for school, something she'd never thought she could do. She'd stood up to a king. Why was she so frightened now?

Because you might love him. Because he's everything good you were afraid to dream of having in your life.

Kat touched her lips, the memory of Logan's kiss, of his arms around her. She'd never forgotten how he made

her feel during that magical week they'd shared. Alive.
Beautiful. Treasured. She'd never felt like that since
she'd walked out that door...until he returned. Offering
her protection. Offering her freedom. Offering himself.

Logan had saved her and their children. He said he
wanted her. Every part of her longed to be with him.
To see if the magic was real. To see if they might make
something beautiful by merging two lives where only
pain existed now. Could she risk it?

How could she not?

Kat lifted her chin, put her hand on the banister and
climbed the stairs, a flutter of excitement starting deep
within. Oh, Lord, she was shaking and he hadn't even
touched her.

But he would.

The second floor was quiet.

Heart beating at a frantic pace, she walked down the
hallway to the children's room. She eased open the door.
They still slept quietly, napping after the strenuous day.
Love for them filled her heart, and she closed them in
with a soft click, knowing her decision about their father was right. They deserved the chance to have him in
their lives...forever. And she wanted the brass ring. For
once in her life, she dared to think she could have it all.

With trembling hands, Kat opened the door to Logan's bedroom, stepped inside, then shut them in.

Logan didn't turn his head, though the tension in his
shoulders told Kat he knew she was there. He sat on the
edge of his bed, a dusty shipping trunk at his feet, the
lid opened, tilting askew. A small box rested on his lap.

"I didn't think you'd come," he said quietly.

Kat crossed the room and sat next to him on the bed,
her thigh touching his. "Gretchen reminded me what

I risked losing," she said. This was not the reception she'd expected.

"Sorry about that. Gretchen has had the run of the ranch for a while and is not famous for holding back her opinions on things."

"No, she's very good at sharing those," Kat said diplomatically, troubled that Logan seemed so distant and closed off again. "I got the impression she knew your mother well."

"They were best friends." Logan pulled a piece of paper from the small box on his lap, then unfolded the letter gently, his hands unsteady.

"I found this note hidden in my mother's desk the day she disappeared," he said, not looking in Kat's direction. "It's not dated, so I don't know when, or how, she planned to give it to me. The letter makes it clear she was leaving my father, at least temporarily."

Kat read the words, written in feminine script, over his shoulder. The letter itself had small imperfections on it, as if tears had dampened the paper, then dried. Logan traced those uneven areas with his finger. Were the tears Logan's or his mother's?

Dearest Logan,
I know the fighting bothers you, and I'm so sorry. I've decided it's best if I leave for a while. Your father needs to cool off, and so do I. Try not to rile him too much.

This ranch is your birthright. I've made sure it's in your name before leaving. Things will work out as they should.

Never doubt that I love you.
Mom

"I couldn't believe she left me or this ranch." Logan sighed and raised his face to the ceiling. "But then she never got away, did she?"

He let the paper drop into the box and set it on the floor. "I had no faith in her, Kat. I was so hurt and angry that I didn't look for her. She would have kept looking for me."

Her heart ached for him. She laid her hand on his cheek. The pain and vulnerability in his eyes scorched her soul, making her own fears seem so petty and selfish.

"She loved you." Kat leaned in and wrapped her arms around him, holding him hard so he would feel her. "Stop torturing yourself. If you'd have known, you would have done something about it. That's the kind of man you are."

Logan stilled. "And what kind of man is that?"

She took a deep breath. "The kind I want to know better. The kind I want to be a father to my children. The kind of man I want to take a risk for."

Vulnerability shadowed the depths of his eyes. "You're certain?"

"No. Yes. I don't know," she choked out with a small laugh. "Actually, I'm scared to death of screwing up. I'm not a good bet, Logan. I have way too many hang-ups. My life is in turmoil. It might be complicated forever if Leopold won't leave us alone. The question is, knowing all that, are you willing to take a chance on me?"

"Yes," he said softly. "For you and my children, I would do anything. We'll take it as slow as you want, and work things out as they come up."

Kat smiled to hide her nervousness. "Then I'm going to call you on your promise from downstairs. I believe that you said if I came in this room, I should not plan on leaving for a while."

"Yes, I remember saying something like that."

"Well, I'm here. Our kids are asleep and I'm not leaving anytime soon."

His smile gave her courage.

She placed her hands on his chest and pushed him back onto the mattress. He let her. She climbed on top of him, her hips settling on his. "I want you to show me," she whispered, leaning down to kiss his lips, "exactly what you had in mind when you threw down that sexual gauntlet."

His eyes went hot with green fire. "With pleasure."

He slid his fingers into the hair at her nape, then tugged her down until her breasts pressed against him and her lips hovered over his. His musky scent intoxicated her and she closed her eyes, breathing in Logan.

"I'm sorry I left," she said, her voice barely above a whisper. "I'm sorry we wasted all that time, when we could have been together."

"Shhh. Concentrate on now. We'll face reality later."

She pressed her mouth to his, then using her tongue and gentle nips on his lower lip, showed him she wanted more. Much more. With a groan he let her inside and the tentative kiss she'd started deepened, slowly heating with an urgency that made her shudder. Her fears melted away and primal instincts kicked in. The rush of excitement thrilled her—each touch, each sound driving her to seek deeper contact.

How had she lived without this? Without him?

Suddenly, he'd flipped her over, tucking her under his hard body. He took over the kiss, teasing her lips apart, exploring her.

Love me now, she begged silently. *Make me believe that we'll be all right.*

His hands went everywhere, and she reveled in his touch.

She slid his buttons free, then shoved his shirt aside to feel the bare skin beneath. Her hand encountered tape and a large white bandage covering part of his shoulder. She stilled under him. "What happened?"

"Gunshot," Logan said. "I'm fine. Just a scratch."

Her passion-hazed brain cleared. "When?"

"Leaving the hotel. The bodyguard got me."

"You drove all the way here with an untreated bullet wound?" She lay back against the pillows. "You could have died."

He captured her gaze and smiled. "It's just a little tender, Kat. It'll be healed in a few days."

"You were shot because of me."

"Don't ever think that. Considering what I got as a result of coming back into your life—you and the twins— that's worth a little blood. I definitely can't complain."

He nibbled at her lower lip, his hand teasing the hem of her shirt with featherlight caresses. Kat's body melted beneath his. He kissed both eyes, both cheeks and settled on her mouth.

Kat was lost. She couldn't think. She could only feel. Her arms hugged him tighter and he shifted his hips against hers. His hands paused at the buttons of her jeans.

"Any doubts?"

"About the future, God, yes. About this? Not a one. Now hurry."

He grinned and slowly lowered the zipper.

DEKE POWELL COULDN'T BELIEVE he sat here, hiding out in the dirt between a grove of oak trees on Logan Carmichael's ranch in "end-of-the-earth," Texas. Powell blew on his hands to warm them up, then slipped his gloves back on, grabbed his gun and binoculars again, and scanned the bustle of activity.

Victor's people had told him this place should be nearly deserted, but from what he could see of the construction site, every law-enforcement officer within fifty miles was crawling over the property. How was Deke supposed to plant the explosives and get away? But that was the assignment so he'd better figure it out soon.

He cursed Hans for getting him into this mess, not that Deke would ever be anything but subservient to the man. Hans was a psycho and he had a direct line to Victor.

Deke wasn't a killer, though, and he didn't want to harm those two small children, but he couldn't let himself think about that. He couldn't think about anything but Maria's horrific scream when that bastard, Victor, had cut off her finger.

He glanced at his watch. Out of time. Somehow, he'd have to use the chaos at the construction site to his advantage. He might have to wait until dark. Deke grabbed his bag of explosives, but before he moved, a distinctive ringtone sounded in his ear. He glanced at the phone's screen and his throat went dry.

"Maria?" he whispered. "Are you okay, honey?"

"Of course she's okay," a taunting voice rushed out. "We were just having a little fun, were we not, my dear? You're a lucky man, Deke. She's a sweet one."

Deke's knuckles whitened as he gripped a branch from the tree. His jaw tightened. "You do anything else to hurt her—"

"And what? You'll kill me? You should know better than to threaten me."

Deke froze, praying the man wouldn't cut off another

of Maria's fingers in retaliation. "I'm sorry." He spat out the words from between clenched teeth.

"That's better," the man said silkily. "And remember…don't do anything stupid. I'm aware of your every move."

Impotent fury welled inside him, but Deke kept the challenge from his voice. "I'll get the job done."

"Yes," his boss said, as another of Maria's screams sounded in the background. "I believe you will. We'll talk soon."

Despair swept through Deke and the gun trembled in his hand. He couldn't think about what was happening to Maria or he'd go insane. Why had he ever agreed to work with Victor? He didn't care who sat on the throne in Bellevaux.

Deke hung his head. He knew why he'd taken the job. It had seemed like easy money at first. When Hans had approached him, Deke had thought he could do the things they asked without a problem. They'd offered too much tax-free cash to pass up after he and Maria had been laid off. He hadn't cared about the group's politics or their agenda. All they'd wanted him to do was a little surveillance. A quick exchange of information in a back alley. He'd been a fool.

One job led to another, each successively shadier, uglier, more dangerous. Until now, his complicity in the crimes against the royal court would lead to a death sentence for treason. Yet, when he'd tried to quit, he'd realized all too quickly Maria would pay the price.

Deke only prayed the terrorists hadn't discovered her pregnancy. She was a little over three months. A prospective birth should bring joy, not this bone-chilling fear. How had his life gone so wrong? All he could do now was plan the latest massacre the group had decreed.

The only person who might be able to help him…
well, he could never ask.

A half hour later, heavy steps pounded behind him.
Gripping his gun, Deke whirled around, ready to fire.

Hans. The psycho scared the hell out of him. His
knife sheath was bloodstained. Apparently Hans's shoulder wound wasn't slowing him down from his favorite
pastime. The killing had begun. There was no going
back.

Hans sifted through the bag, then met Deke's gaze
with a satisfied grin. "A lot of people will die today. I
like your plan."

"So glad, because this is a two-man job," Deke bit out.

"Which is why I'm here. That, and to keep you in
line." Hans ran some fine grit across the bloodied surface of his knife until the blade shone clean. He sighed
and held up the knife, turning it, and watched the serrated edge glinting in the sunlight. "I love this knife. It's
too bad we're using explosives. They're so impersonal."

Deke stared at the blade, certain he'd be the next one
to feel the bite of its steel, if things didn't go as planned.
"It's time to go."

The man smiled and ran his finger near the razor-
sharp edge. "She's already dead, you know."

Deke's heart galloped. "What do you mean?"

"Your wife." Hans raised his head and looked at Deke
with soul-dead eyes. "The minute you finish this job,
Victor *will* kill her. He never leaves witnesses."

LOGAN COULDN'T GET enough of Kat's bare skin. He
needed to touch her, to make her his. To prove to himself once and for all that she belonged to him.

Part of him couldn't believe she'd walked up those
stairs instead of running out the door with one child

under each arm. He should've known better. Kat didn't run from much—except herself.

He let his fingers explore her silky legs, too long to be real. Midday light illuminated her alabaster skin as he stroked the softness on the inside of her knee. She shifted her legs, parting them a bit, begging for another touch. His lips followed his fingertips, kissing then tasting her as he worked his way down her limbs.

Her lavender scent intoxicated him. He could lose himself in the enthralling aroma that was only Kat. Slowly, he explored back up, past her calves to her thighs. When his hand reached the silk panties covering her, Kat moaned.

"Logan, please. It's too much."

He nipped at the lace beneath her belly button, then lifted his gaze. Her ice-blue eyes blazed with heat.

"Should I stop?" He raised his head slightly, moving his body away from hers.

"Don't you dare."

He chuckled and left the lace, then explored the nip of her waist until he settled on the full curve of her breasts, still hidden from his gaze. He flicked open the front clasp of her bra, revealing the beauty beneath. His chest tightened. "You're more than I remember. Sweeter, lovelier, more responsive."

"I've had two babies." She touched a stretch mark on her belly.

"My babies," he said softly, and kissed the slightly whitened skin.

He divested her of the final scraps of lace, and she lay before him. The mother of his children. A woman he wanted more than anything.

He crawled beside her, pushing his thigh between her legs. Her eyes widened. She could feel his obvious response to her. He longed to lose himself in her, to forget the outside world, but he wanted more.

For her.

From her.

He pushed the blond hair out of her eyes and drew his finger down her arm. For a moment he just looked at her. Her tongue bathed her lips and they glistened, beckoning him. He shivered.

"Aren't you going to make love to me?" she whispered, her voice husky.

He traced her arm to her breasts and touched a beaded nipple. She couldn't stop a low moan from escaping her. He arched against her. "You know I want you."

She returned the favor, squirming against him, and his heartbeat raced under the touch of fingertips as they teased his chest.

He clasped her hands and held them above her head, shifting over her. He settled his hips into the cradle of hers. Her breathing turned shallow. He let her legs part. With just a push, he could enter her softness, become a part of her.

He wanted everything.

"Stay with me," he said. "I want you here with me. Always."

"Logan, can't we talk about this later?"

She nipped at his chest, scraping across his hypersensitive skin with her teeth. He let out a low groan. He didn't move, and laid his head beside hers, releasing her hands. "I can't take someone else leaving me. Not now."

The moment the confession escaped his lips, he regretted revealing his vulnerability. She stilled and stroked his head before kissing his cheek and wrapping her arms and legs around him.

"I walked up those stairs, didn't I?"

She tilted her hips to his. With a groan he reached into the bedside table for a foil packet and donned the protection before sliding inside of her.

He groaned as her softness clutched and bound him to her. Slowly, he began to move. With each thrust, Kat gave back, their rhythm age old, but something more, something special. Each movement wound them tighter and tighter, merging them together into one soul, one harmony.

He rocked against her, the ecstasy between them, Kat holding on and crying out his name as she shuddered beneath him, tiny pulses driving him to distraction.

Unable to resist, in one last thrust, he reached completion.

He sagged on top of her. Never before had he felt this way. He kissed Kat's temple. She opened her baby blues, her eyes glistening with satisfaction, and more. Tenderness, hope, trust.

He didn't want to move away from her. His entire being dripped with contentment, and then the truth hit him with the force of a west Texas tornado.

He was home. Kat *was* his home.

A SUDDEN WEIGHT LANDED on top of Logan, shocking him from sleep. His eyelids flew open and he managed to quell his instinctive defensive reaction in time not to harm the wriggling kid that had jumped on him. He stared at Hayden's smiling face and laughed, before his son proceeded to climb all over him.

"Get up, Daddy. We's hungry."

Lanie looked at him curiously from the bedside. "What are you and Mommy doing?"

Quickly, he looked down, relieved to see he'd tucked the blankets over him and Kat before they'd fallen asleep in each other's arms. This situation could still be tricky, but at least there was no necessity for a talk about the birds and the bees with overly curious two-and-a-half-year-olds. "We were sleeping."

Hayden piped up, "You forgot your jammies!"

Logan grinned at his son. "So I did."

He grabbed Hayden as the little boy was about to pounce on Kat. "Hey, careful buddy. Mommy's sleeping."

Kat lifted her head and peered at them blearily. "Not anymore." She rolled over and tugged the covers tightly across her body. "Nap time is supposed to be for another half hour."

Logan forced himself to look at the kids sternly. "What are you doing up?"

Hayden plopped down on Logan's stomach again. "It's too noisy outside. Nap time is all done. I want juice."

"And how about you, sweet girl? You hungry, too?" Kat asked Lanie, her eyes wide and solemn.

Logan reached out and touched her nose. "What's the matter? You look worried."

She bit her lip. "I found something shiny," she said. "It's in my pocket. Are you going to take it away again?"

Logan's heart raced. The last thing Lanie had found had been his mother's locket. "I don't know, honey. I'll have to see what it is. Can you show me?"

Silently, Lanie pulled a silver horseshoe from her pocket. "I like it," she said. "It's pretty."

Logan looked at the vintage Christmas ornament clutched in her chubby hand. "Where did you find it?"

"In that box." Lanie pointed to the shipping trunk.

There was a small keepsake box, full of Christmas ornaments, next to the stationery kit holding his mother's letter. It seemed to be a day for memories.

He fingered the tattered ribbon that his mother had used to hang the horseshoe ornament on the tree. He'd locked it away after she disappeared. They'd been handed down, generation after generation, as part of the Carmichael legacy. He hadn't wanted his father to ruin them like he'd ruined everything else. Would she be happy to know her granddaughter seemed to share that same love for her treasures?

Hayden pushed closer, checking out the horseshoe. "Lanie likes shiny things. But she takes them without p'mission. She's naughty."

Logan raised his brow. "I seem to remember a certain little boy going outside when he wasn't supposed to. We'll have to work more on that permission stuff. Okay, hotshot?"

Logan tickled Hayden, who collapsed in a fit of giggles. Kat smiled.

"Lanie, can I show you something?" Logan placed his palm out toward the little girl.

She nodded, but handed her prize over very reluctantly.

"My great-great-*great*-grandmother believed this land was lucky. She had this horseshoe Christmas ornament made to celebrate when her first baby was born. She believed good luck would always follow the family as long as we stayed on the ranch. That's why I use a horseshoe as my brand."

Hayden frowned. "What's a brand?"

Okay, talking about putting a hot piece of metal on a steer's rump might be a lot more complicated than Logan wanted to explain.

Lanie saved him. "It's s'posta go on a Christmas tree?"

Logan nodded. "It certainly does."

"Our Christmas tree is broken." Lanie bowed her head. "It fell down and now I can't find it. I think it's lost or frowed away."

Logan tilted his daughter's chin up and stared into her sad eyes. "Then what do you say we find a new tree to decorate?"

"Can the kitties help us?" Hayden asked. "I didn't get to play with them today."

Logan glanced over at Kat, who tried hard not to laugh. "Yeah, sure. Maybe some of the kitties can play in a cardboard box while they watch us."

He could just hear Gretchen pitching a fit about barn cats in the house. He shook his head. He didn't care. He had his family. On his ranch. Right where they were supposed to be.

Chapter Eight

Logan walked down the front porch stairs. He'd send a couple of men for a tree, then head over to the well. The crime-scene tape and a raised tarp still protected the area, but the crowd of law enforcement and vehicles had thinned.

Blake came around the edge of the house and intercepted Logan on the way to the barn. "I assume things are going better since you've been gone for over an hour and I saw the ghost of a smile on your face a minute ago?"

To Logan's amazement, his cheeks warmed. "Yeah, things are looking up."

Blake smiled, but even that was bittersweet. "You deserve something good to happen, my friend. Things have been tough for a while. Maybe today's a turning point."

"I hope so." Logan called over his foreman, then pulled out a bunch of bills from his wallet. "Grab Tim and run into town. Pick up a Christmas tree with all the trimmings."

The foreman's hand froze in the process of taking the money, staring at Logan. "Christmas? Here? We haven't done that since—"

"Since my mother disappeared. I know," Logan interrupted.

Blake looked at Logan. "Christmas?"

He scuffed his boot in the dirt. "Lanie wants a tree for Christmas, and she's going to get it."

"No problem, boss." The foreman nabbed Tim and the two men jumped into a pickup and barreled toward the front gate.

Blake rocked back on his heels. "Well, I'd say that's definitely a turning point."

"Every kid deserves a Christmas."

"I'm not arguing with you, buddy."

"Would you..." Logan hesitated, feeling awkward with these unfamiliar urges to act like a real father. "Would you, Amanda and Ethan come over to help us decorate? I might need some moral support."

"Count on it." Blake's voice made it clear he understood the situation all too well.

Logan was happy now, but things could change all too quickly.

He shoved down the tumult of feelings at thinking there would finally be a joyful holiday celebration at the ranch. Christmas, with his family. He never would have believed it possible. He met Blake's understanding gaze, then looked away. He needed answers. "So, what's the status with the investigation?"

Shifting into law-enforcement mode, Blake straightened his stance. "Most of the crews are done, but they're still taking some of the dirt and debris from the bottom of the well to check for forensic evidence that may have been buried over time. They'll sift through it and maybe we'll get lucky."

An eerie feeling suddenly flowed over Logan, almost as if he were being watched. He looked around, trying to account for the unexplained sense of danger. "Excuse me a minute." He took out his phone and dialed. "Rafe?

Assign extra guards around the property, even more than I requested before. Something doesn't feel right."

Blake glanced around. "What's going on?"

"I don't know. It might just be all these unfamiliar faces on the property. Obviously, I couldn't vet them all before they came. I upped the security patrols before to make sure none of them came near the house, but my gut is still telling me to watch out."

"I wouldn't discount your instincts. They've saved you often enough before."

"Yeah," Logan said, and gave the land and outbuildings another hard scan before turning back to Blake. "If you don't want to bring your family tonight, Blake…I'd understand."

Blake tilted his Stetson. "You'll still have the patrols up?"

"I'll make sure you get escorted to and from."

"I've never had reason to doubt you, Logan. We'll be here."

"If I get more information, I'll let you know."

Blake squeezed Logan's shoulder. "I know."

"Have you heard from Deputy Parris yet?" Logan asked.

"He said your mother's remains made it safely to the morgue. Debra's there now. She promised to expedite her forensic investigation and get back to you with her findings as soon as possible."

"What does she think, Blake?"

"What are you asking specifically?"

Logan blew out a breath. "Was my mother's cause of death obvious? Did my father kill her?"

Kat's lavender scent wafted over Logan and a moment later, she came up on his right side to stand beside him. She remained silent, but he knew she'd heard his question by the way she rubbed his back gently. Despite his turmoil, her touch comforted him.

"Do you want me to leave so you two can finish?" she asked quietly.

He pulled her closer. "No." He kept his hand over his gun, just in case his instincts were on the mark. "Blake was just giving me an update."

Blake rubbed the nape of his neck. "Debra...Dr. Sandoval did a cursory exam on arrival. She said there was significant blunt-force trauma to the back of your mother's skull, but it could have happened when she fell against that sharp rock on the side of the well, or any time during her descent. There were several broken bones, but no evidence of a weapon. So far, the injuries seem consistent with a fall. We may never know what really happened."

Logan swallowed a fresh surge of grief, and Kat pressed tight against his back and wrapped her arms around his waist. Her cheek lay against him and he grasped her hand like a lifeline. "Okay. Thanks for the information."

Logan gestured toward the well. "How much longer will they be here?"

He wanted his ranch back. He wanted to be with Kat and his kids. For a few moments.

"They should be finished in a half hour or so. I've ordered them to cap the well. I hear your little boy is a lively one."

"Hayden has no fear. And that scares the hell out of me. Plus, with the kittens out by the well, it's a big draw to that area."

"The mother cat moved the kittens under the house. She was carrying one under the entrance for the wood box. All the noise and commotion probably scared her."

"That's not going to be much quieter when we refill it with wood for the fireplace," said Logan. He held out his hand to Blake. "Thanks for being here. Thanks for everything."

Blake shook off the compliment. "That's what we do in Carder, Texas. Right? We take care of our own." His cell phone rang and he checked the number. He held up his finger then placed the phone at his ear. "What's up, darlin'?"

While Blake spoke to Amanda, Logan turned in Kat's arms. "Thank you, too."

She shrugged. "For what? I didn't do anything."

He kissed her nose. "You've done more than you know." He wrapped her tight in his arms, rested his chin on her hair and inhaled her sweet scent. He was in deep. For a blessed moment the ugliness of his world disappeared and he just held her.

Blake shoved the cell phone back in its holder. "Well, I'm headed home to handle the latest crisis on the home front. Ethan evidently decided he wanted to ride the tractor again…without his mother's permission. Now, I get to give him what for, to back up his mom." Blake sighed. "Kids. They sure keep things from getting boring."

Logan smiled at long last. "I know what you mean."

Daniel came to, facedown on the filthy stone floor of the dungeon, unable to believe he wasn't dead. God, he'd prayed often enough for it. Grit pressed into his cheek and the smell of his own blood lent a coppery tang to the fetid air. With great effort he tried to move, but searing pain pierced his sides. Damn, how many ribs had they broken?

If he was still alive, he'd somehow missed having a

punctured lung. That was probably the only part of his body still intact.

A clang echoed through the stone hallways like a death toll, and his prison door swung open. Feigning unconsciousness, Daniel peered through nearly swollen closed eyelids to see who would do the honors of beating on him next. Someone new had entered his cell carrying the swill they called food. Beyond him, Daniel could barely make out two guards transporting a man's unmoving body past the open doorway. Blood and bruises mottled every exposed part of the poor guy's skin.

Daniel had lost count of how many people the duke had sadistically tortured and watched die. Sick bastard.

Only one prisoner remained at that end of the hallway. The only one to have survived longer than Daniel. He didn't know how the duke had dared keep the man alive so long.

Daniel waited for the final sound of his own door slamming shut.

Silence.

His stomach roiled. Did the duke intend to come back to finish the job? Daniel had told them nothing they didn't already know.

An older man in a guard's uniform stood there with a plate, watching Daniel and listening to the noises in the dungeon. The guard pushed the cell door nearly shut and ventured closer. His steps frightened away the rats that had begun circling Daniel. The man knelt next to him, and he pressed two fingers against Daniel's neck, looking for a pulse.

"I'll kill you," Daniel growled as he grabbed the man by the throat, then collapsed in horrific agony as his shattered body failed him.

"Stop! I'm here to help you," the man whispered. "They mustn't hear."

The guard's words reached Daniel through the threatening darkness.

"How?" he asked, forcing the words through cracked lips.

"The Falcon knows you're here."

Noah? Daniel gasped as he struggled for a breath. *Had Logan sent him?*

"Can you walk?"

He stared into the man's sympathetic eyes. "I don't know."

The guard nodded. "If you're alive in twenty-four hours, there might be a way out. Be ready."

A man's heavy footsteps marched on the stone walkway.

The guard cursed and rose. Before he could leave the cell, the duke blocked the doorway.

"What are you doing with this prisoner?" he snapped.

"I—I brought his food in," the man stuttered, "but I thought he was dead, your Grace. I was checking for a pulse."

Sarbonne stepped closer. "Is he dead?"

"N-No, Your Grace."

"What is your name?"

"P-Pierre Thomas, your Grace."

The man bowed low, then moved uncertainly toward the door. "May I go now?"

"*You* may come with me," the duke said, pulling his whip from his belt. "We need to have a chat."

Daniel sent up a prayer for the man who may have forfeited his life to bring that message of hope. Hope. Something Daniel had given up on a dozen beatings ago. He had to stay alive.

He heard the crack of the whip and the old man's agonized cry.

Daniel flinched, and a strange warmth stung his eyes as he lay his battered cheek against the cold stones. Twenty-four more hours. Somehow, he had to stay alive.

He didn't know what Noah's escape plan would entail, but Daniel prayed the old guard and the prisoner down the hall could survive one more day.

Daniel didn't intend to leave anyone behind.

KAT LOOKED AROUND THE living room that Logan had turned into a Christmas postcard and smiled through happy tears. An enormous tree filled one corner of the room, and the twins ran back and forth carrying the latest ornament to hang on its branches. The joy in their faces stunned her. She had never seen them this happy, and watching Logan lift them in his arms to reach the highest spots melted her heart. *This* is what she'd dreamed of, and never believed she could have. Logan had made it all possible. Her heart swelled with love and she wished that life could always stay this happy.

She carried the bowl of popcorn to where Gretchen and Blake's wife, Amanda, sat stringing popcorn and cranberries. Kat crossed her legs and eased down onto the floor to join them. She placed the bowl in the center, where they all could reach, and grabbed a needle already threaded with string.

Across the room the sheriff and his five-year-old son, Ethan, helped Hayden place snowflake ornaments on the large evergreen tree. The room was filled with laughter. Egg nog and hot chocolate flowed freely, and Christmas carols played from the stereo.

She grabbed a handful of popcorn and tossed it in her mouth.

Amanda nudged her. "Hey, stop eating the decorations."

Kat laughed, relaxing fully for the first time since coming back in the house with Logan. "I can't tell you how much it means that you and Blake and Ethan came over. It just makes tonight that much more special."

Gretchen smiled at her and lifted her hot chocolate in a toast. "To smart women. It's nice to find three of us all in one room."

Kat blushed, knowing Gretchen had played a big part in this family gathering becoming a reality. Kat blessed the woman's Irish temper.

Amanda nodded toward Lanie and Logan. "Your little one doesn't leave his side for an instant, does she?"

"He's her hero," Kat said softly, watching the picturesque scene.

"Logan's a good man," Amanda said. "I watched him sacrifice almost everything for me and Ethan when we were in trouble. He didn't even question Blake when he asked for help. I don't know what we would have done without him."

"They grow them good in Carder, don't they?" Kat said, staring at Logan inspecting the latest ornament Lanie brought him.

Gretchen sighed. "That they do. You young ladies would know more about that than most as you've snagged two of the best for yourselves. And, from the heated ways they've been looking at you two tonight, I've no doubt there will be more wee ones running around here in the future."

Amanda flushed and met Kat's gaze. She lowered her head. Logan did know his way around a woman's body, and from Amanda's expression as she smiled at her husband, so did Blake.

Hayden giggled as he showed Ethan how to work the siren on his toy fire engine. They flicked the siren on and off until Kat suggested they find something different to play with for a while. The boys hunkered down with a couple of toys Ethan had brought with him.

Blake and Logan walked over to the group of women, and Blake leaned down to kiss his wife. "It's getting late, and I have an early start tomorrow. Are you ready to go?"

Amanda nodded and added her completed cranberry strand to the pile ready to go on the tree. "It was nice meeting you, Kat. You have a beautiful family."

"So do you," Kat said, as Blake helped his wife to her feet.

They called to Ethan.

Lanie came over, too, and held tight to Logan's leg, her shyness still in evidence as she watched the other family prepare to leave.

"I'll let you know when I hear something," Blake said to Logan when everyone had donned their coats and hats.

"Thanks," Logan said, sending Lanie back to Kat before turning toward the door.

Blake hesitated. "By the way, how's that intuition doing?"

Their gazes met.

"Still screaming louder than I'd like," Logan said quietly. "You notice all the blinds are pulled down tight and the lamps strategically placed to not throw shadows on the windows? The ranch is on lockdown after you leave. The men will escort you out, but even with extra patrol, I'm not taking chances. Zane picked up some irregularities in the security system that I don't like."

Blake nodded. "Take care of your family."

"I intend to," Logan said. "You do the same."

A few minutes after, the Redmonds left, the house was locked and the alarm set. Gretchen headed to her room, and Logan sank down into the leather sofa next to Kat. The children played on the floor.

Logan tried to keep his mind off the report he'd received from Zane. Noah Bradford suspected Daniel may be held captive by terrorists. The story gave credence to the theory that his captors had used Daniel's explosives expertise to frame him. The worst part, though, made Logan's stomach turn. If Daniel had been held all this time, then Logan had left him to die by not searching for him. Just like his mother. He shuddered and pinched the bridge of his nose. So many variables. Hopefully Noah would have the answer. And soon.

Kat leaned against the warmth of his body and cuddled closer. "What are you thinking?"

Logan welcomed the distraction of her softness. He kissed her lips gently.

That I won't let anything happen to you. You or the kids.

"I'm thinking that a pair of almost three-year-olds have utterly exhausted me," Logan lied, hugging her to him. "That I never thought I'd be here with you. With them. And, I never thought I'd have this." He swept his hand across the idyllic scene. "All of it."

Kat tilted her head and stared into his eyes. "But are you truly happy?"

"Yes." He pushed the hair back from her face. "I've always wanted a family, but I never imagined it could be this good. I am truly happy."

She smiled and leaned closer. "Me, too."

Lanie tugged at Kat's jeans. "Mommy, we forgot the

shiny horseshoe for the tree. It's in my pocket." Lanie pulled the treasured ornament out.

"Oh, no, what shall we do?" Logan cried dramatically, sweeping Lanie into his arms with a flourish. "We can't forget the most important ornament of all."

She giggled.

He lifted her high. "Should it go at the top?"

"No, Daddy. The tree's too big. I wanna see it."

He set her down in front of the tree. Carefully, Lanie hung the generations-old ornament between two candy canes on the lower branches. She stepped back, proud.

Kat crossed the room. "That looks perfect, Lanie."

Hayden rolled his fire engine across their feet and flipped the siren on again.

"I think it's time for two kids to go to bed," Kat said.

The twins protested and Lanie ran over for one last visit to the tree, but soon Logan and Kat had them bathed and in bed. After a story and water and a bit more whining, Kat closed the door behind her. "Lanie will be out like a light in no time. Hayden, on the other hand—"

"Yeah. I get the impression he's going to be a night owl. I can't believe he dismantled the baby monitor after his nap. Zane said he'd have it back to us tomorrow, *if* we can find the rest of the pieces."

"If not, we'll buy another one. I need to know what's going on with Hayden at all times."

"He won't get up and get out, will he? Isn't he afraid of the dark?"

"Hayden," Kat insisted, "is not afraid of anything."

"I guess you're right. After supper, Gretchen found him hiding in the wood box attached to the house. The shed opens to the outside and to the kitchen."

"I never heard of anything like that."

"It's great for storing wood in winter. You use the

outside door for loading wood, and the kitchen one for getting firewood without having to go out in the cold. The outside door is kept locked, but the wood box is still pretty dark and scary."

"Why would Hayden go in there?"

"He was trying to jimmy the outside lock to visit the kittens. Apparently, he wanted to play with them. Gretchen said he almost had the door open. I'm going to have to get a dead bolt to keep him in."

"God, he really is a little Houdini," Kat muttered in frustration.

"Okay, enough kid talk. It's time for a grown-up question." Logan held out his hand. "What'll it be? Stay here or my room?"

"What a sexy proposal." She laughed. "Do you have to ask?"

"You want sexy? How's this?" He swept her in his arms and carried her the short walk to his bedroom. Once inside, he kicked the door shut. After sliding her down his body, he started removing her blouse. "Better?"

"Much."

When his lips caressed her shoulder, Kat sighed. "I think we'd better lock the door. We're going to be doing some things that little eyes should not see."

Logan laughed. "I promise we will be."

Logan's cell phone vibrated in his pocket. He pulled it out and cursed. "It's King Leopold."

Kat sighed. "Do you think he's decided to leave us alone?"

"If he hasn't," Logan said with a growl, "then Zane's information about Leopold's rare earth metal dealings ought to make him think twice." Logan pushed the speakerphone. "Your Majesty."

"Get my daughter on the phone now," Leopold barked.

"Kat's right here and you're on speakerphone. She can hear every word."

The king huffed. "Katherine, I've had enough of your stonewalling. The situation here is growing desperate. You must listen to me. Come to Bellevaux now and bring your son. It's imperative you leave immediately. I sent my private jet back for you. You could be here by morning."

"No."

"Dammit, woman. I'll give you whatever you want. Houses, cars, jewelry. Anything you desire, but you *must* come now. This week. We're out of time."

"Why won't you listen to me? I'm *not* a princess, I never wanted to be and I never will be."

"Katherine—"

She cut him off. "And one more thing, Your Majesty, I have two children. A son *and* a daughter, and I have a life in this country. Find someone else to be your heir."

"There *is* no one else! This country will cease to exist if you don't become my heir before Christmas."

"I'm illegitimate. Even if I wanted to, I wouldn't be accepted by your people."

The king cleared his throat. "My great-great-grandfather was a bit adventurous. When he had a child out of wedlock, his father changed the law. All you have to do is agree for me to adopt you, and you and your children *will* be legitimate."

"If that king could change a law, then you do it, too. Make up a law that will work. I'm an adult. I'm not going to be adopted by a man who doesn't want me."

"I didn't know you existed until your mother sent your birth certificate and some photographs in the mail."

"What? She would never do that."

Leopold cursed. "I don't have time to argue with you about it. I don't know whether or not she had second thoughts, but by the time I tracked her down, she'd passed away."

Kat's head swam. Her mother had lied all that time, then sent Kat's birth certificate to the king when she realized she was dying? "How did you find me?"

"I hired Logan three years ago."

"Three years?" Her gaze met Logan's. "I was your... *assignment?*" She hissed. "The chance meeting? The instant attraction? It was a setup? All of it?"

Oh, God. It was true. She could see it in his eyes.

She couldn't breathe. Couldn't think. "Has everyone been lying to me all along? My mother. My father...and you? Was any of it real?"

Logan reached for her, but she stepped away from him. Oh, God, she couldn't breathe. Her knees shook. "Did he hire you to sleep with me, too, or were the extra heirs a bonus? I hope you got paid."

"Katherine, don't be crude. We don't have time for this."

Logan grabbed the phone. "She's not coming back, Leopold. And if you call again, that secret deal you've set up with your friends from Russia and Yemen will become public knowledge. I'll make sure the right people hear about it. Do I make myself clear?"

The king sputtered and Logan hung up.

He thrust his hand through his hair. "I was going to tell you—"

"When? Obviously not before we went to bed and had hot sex for a week. It's amazing how that never entered into our discussions about your job description. I believe you said you were a rancher?"

"I am."

She shook her head. "You're so much more than that, though. Aren't you?"

"It didn't bother you a half hour ago."

"And, it wouldn't have mattered now if you'd told me the truth when we met, Logan. But you didn't bother. You just lied."

"I can't change what's happened."

Why didn't he tell her it was all a mistake?

Logan stepped toward her. She backed away. "I need room. I can't breathe."

He stilled. "I didn't know you were his daughter, but he did hire me to find you."

She stared at the ground. "We didn't just run into each other. You knew who I was. You were paid. Whatever you told him must have been impressive. He never contacted me."

"I told him where you worked. What you did for a living. That's it, Kat. What happened between us was real."

She snapped her head up and glared. "Nothing was real about that week, Logan. Nothing."

"We have two children together, Kat. You can't just walk away from that. You might still be in danger."

"I'm not walking away. I know I'm still in trouble and I won't risk my children's lives because I'm angry and hurt. But I want Rafe to watch over me. Not you. Everything I believed about my life has been thrown up in the air and my future threatened by other people who thought lying to me was for my own good. I need to make some decisions on my own. I'll let you know what they are."

She left his room and went into the guest room next to the kids'.

Kat sank to the floor and she let the tears fall.

She'd almost had it all. Now she had to figure out what was left.

THE FIRST RAYS OF daylight broke over the frost-covered hills. What a night. The extra guards had played havoc with his plans, but he and Hans had finally finished setting the charges.

Deke hated to see the dawn, knowing what he was about to do. Innocent people would be killed and he couldn't figure a way out of it. Maria's life was forfeit if he failed. According to Hans, even if Deke succeeded she might not survive. His hands shook as, for the hundredth time, he verified the connections on the electronic controller that would set off the explosions.

"Would you quit playing with that thing," Hans muttered, scanning the property with the binoculars. "You're taking forever."

"It takes as long as it takes," Deke bit out. "Did you place everything exactly like I told you."

Hans yawned. "Of course, and I took out three of Carmichael's guards. I don't know why we can't just shoot them all and be done with it."

"Because the boss wants this place decimated. Evidently Carmichael screwed up some special deal in Uzbekistan a couple years ago."

"Carmichael killed Victor's son. No wonder." Hans whistled. "How do you know all this?"

Deke froze in place. He couldn't let slip that Maria's father was a loyalist and part of the underground resisting the Duke of Sarbonne's attempted takeover. If the terrorists knew of her link, Maria would be tortured for that information, as well. "It's my job to know. Did you hide the bodies of the men you killed?"

"Most of them." Hans spit on the ground. "It's not going to matter in a minute. There will be body parts flying everywhere."

Despite the cold temperature outside, sweat rolled down Deke's back. He couldn't stall much longer or Hans would figure out that Deke half hoped someone *would* find a body and sound an alarm. He didn't want to press that detonator.

After today, he would be a murderer.

He thought of the two young children he'd seen the day before and shuddered. But, if he didn't go through with this, his own child might not have a chance to live.

"Hold on. What's that movement near the house?" Hans put the binoculars to his eyes and smiled. "Check it out. The rest of the kills may not be so impersonal, after all."

Deke squinted. A blond-headed little boy peeked out of a small doorway on the side of the house. Deke remembered breaking the lock on the outer door of the little shed full of wood. It had been a great place for a few explosives to keep the chain going.

He clenched his fists as he watched the child climb over the wood pile and jump down before walking across the yard toward the bull pen. The boy had something red and white clutched in his hand. Had he disrupted the explosives?

Guilt washed through Deke. The boy wouldn't have escaped if Deke hadn't broken that lock.

Hans laughed, drawing out his knife. "Could this get any better, or what? I get to kill a royal rugrat today. But I want to play with him first."

"Hans. No!" Before Deke could stop the psycho, Hans sprinted across the field, the sun glinting off the deadly blade in his fist.

A moment later, a young man opened the barn door to Hans's left. The ranch hand reached for his gun, but Hans was on him before he could fire. They wrestled, and the man managed to yell, "Hayden, run!"

His cry turned into a garbled scream as Hans slit the man's throat in one motion then turned toward the boy.

Hans grabbed the kid, clamped a hand over his mouth and ran toward the outlying buildings where Deke hid. "Blow it. Now!"

Deke's stomach churned. He couldn't do this.

The little boy kicked and scratched like a wild-cat. With one hand, Hans ripped the detonator out of Deke's grasp and slammed the button down. "Let's get out of here."

It was done. The countdown had started. Within five minutes this whole place would explode. Stunned, he watched Hans take off with the boy, knowing he planned to torture the child. Deke couldn't do it. He couldn't let Hans kill the boy.

A Sig Sauer clutched in Deke's fingers, he ran toward them. He had to stop Hans. There had to be another way to end this nightmare.

The boy bit Hans and the big man threw the child to the ground and raised his knife.

Blood roared in Deke's ears. He couldn't let this happen. Not even for Maria.

The arc of the knife swung down.

"No!" Deke raised his weapon and pulled the trigger.

Hans jerked and fell to the ground.

The boy got up and ran, but Deke couldn't move.

Chapter Nine

At the sound of the gunshot, Logan bolted upright in the chair in the guest room where he'd held vigil over Kat. He shook her awake. "Grab the kids. You're going to the panic room."

Streaks of dawn slipped through the window shutters, giving him just enough light to see the shock register on her face. "What happened?"

"Gunshot. Move it."

She threw back the covers and hopped out of bed, tugging on her jeans and sweatshirt over the T-shirt she'd worn to bed. He pressed a button on his cell phone. "Rafe? What's going on?"

"We've been compromised. At least three men down. Two dead."

A sharp curse escaped Logan. "How?"

"The accident. The kid's tires didn't blow. They were shot out. It was a diversion to take down the fence and sensors."

Logan's mind whirled. "It takes some pretty sophisticated equipment to detect our sensors."

"Zane called. They entered on the most vulnerable side of the ranch. The ravines and dry creek bed provide natural hideouts. They took out the patrols there. According to the survivor, there's at least two men, and one has a serrated knife," Rafe added meaningfully.

Logan's blood chilled. Paulina's killer. "Find them."

Logan disconnected and grabbed Kat. "Move. Now."

They raced down the hall. He pushed open the door to see Lanie asleep and his son gone. His heart stopped. "Hayden!"

He scared Lanie awake, but Hayden didn't appear. Logan whipped the baby out of bed, along with her pink blanket and shoved her into Kat's arms. "Take Lanie to the panic room. I'll find Hayden."

Kat bolted for the stairs, while Logan ran from room to room. The second floor was deserted. He did a quick sweep downstairs and headed into the kitchen.

Gretchen hovered near the window, peering out. "Was that a gunshot?" she asked.

"We have a security breach," Logan said quickly, moving to check the house alarm, which was still armed. "Have you seen Hayden?"

Her face paled. "No."

"He's got to be here somewhere."

Kat hurried over to him, clutching their daughter. "Gretchen can take Lanie. I'll help you look."

"No!" Logan said. "You should already be in the panic room. Everyone go. *Now.*"

Armed with his Glock, Logan did a quick check of the windows near the stairwell then motioned for them to follow him downstairs. Zane was shoving movable carts of electronics into the panic room and locking everything down.

Logan ushered them in. "Hayden's missing," he told Zane. "Run a heat scan on the house and outside."

Zane raced to one of the units and tapped the keys. "Scanning."

"What the hell happened?"

"Whoever did this is good." Zane's face was red with fury. "They looped video through the cameras to look live. I'm not sure if someone inside didn't help them get the footage."

"If he did, we'll find him dead. These guys don't leave people behind," Logan said.

Zane hit a few more buttons and studied the monitor. "No heat signature in or near the house, just the cats underneath.... Wait a minute." He pointed at a blank spot on the electronic map of the house. "The sensor on the outside wood box door is not responding. Does Hayden know about the shed?"

Logan swore. "I caught him in there yesterday. He heard meowing. The shed is right above the cat's new nest for her litter."

"If he unlocked the kitchen access door, he's small enough to crawl over the wood. That door—" Zane indicated the dark sensor "—leads to the outside..." His voice trailed off.

Kat gasped. "Hayden could be anywhere."

"I'll find him." Logan rounded on Zane. "Get the security systems back up. I want audio and video STAT."

"Take this." Zane handed Logan an earpiece. "I switched channels. There's no way to monitor them, even if they've taken an earpiece from one of our missing men."

Logan turned to Kat and pulled her into his arms, working to wipe the terrified expression from her face, but knowing only Hayden's return would slow the pounding of her heart. "I'll find him. Lock yourself inside."

"Let me help."

"I need to know you're safe. I can't be distracted."

She bit her lip and grabbed his arm. "Find our son."

Logan leaned in and kissed her, tasting her desperation. "He'll be back for a 'time out' before you know it. Take care of Lanie." He punched the code and the panic room's steel door slowly began to close. "Don't leave until I give the all clear. No matter what you see or hear."

With one last look at the woman he'd grown to love, he rushed up the stairs. The kitchen access door to the wood box was unlocked and he peered through the small shed and saw daylight. Cursing, he ran out the front door. Dawn had barely broken through the sky, and most of the regular ranch hands hadn't arrived yet. Thank goodness.

He tapped the headset. "Everything secure inside?"

"Affirmative."

"Any sign of Hayden? The wood box is open."

"No, but I don't trust the camera feeds. I've identified three so far that were compromised. On the west end of the property leading up to the house. I'll keep trying."

"Pull most of the guards to the house. Keep the ranch hands away. And maintain contact."

Logan scanned his property as he rounded the house to the woodshed. The outside lock had been tampered with, and he could see where Hayden had displaced the wood climbing out.

He glanced under the house, and, to his surprise, the kittens were gone. Where the hell would they go now? Hayden must be looking for them. He cupped his hands around his mouth. "Hayden? Are you out here?"

Dread surged within him. Between the barns and construction area, there were too many places for a little boy to hide.

The bull snorted from behind the fence. Surely his son wouldn't have—

An explosion rocked the ground as one of the outbuildings blew. The hot rush of air slammed Logan to the dirt.

Shooting fire arced over him, pelting his back with burning debris. He dragged off his coat as another fireball lit the dawn sky. Logan stumbled to his feet. Panic tore at his heart. "Hayden!"

The distant sound of a car engine roared and Logan ran toward it. The noise grew fainter.

He ran past the propane tank and a blinking flash of red caught his eye. Another bomb! The pace of the blinking quickened.

"Hayden!" He tore through the site, yelling for everyone who appeared to get down.

The tower blew. Fire surged like a hungry beast, decimating everything it touched. The inferno rose higher than the barn roof. Billowing smoke poured out from the tank making the world hazy.

Screams of the wounded assaulted him as he frantically searched for his son. Soot and ash stung his eyes. Then, to his left, another explosion rocked the barn. Shards of wood and metal bombarded the surrounding buildings.

Before Logan could catch his breath, to his right, a series of four more detonations turned the old buildings and the ones under construction into splinters.

This wasn't just an attempt to kill Kat and his children. This was much, much more. Victor. The only man who wanted to destroy him. Heart and soul.

Rafe's truck barreled through the smoke. The vehicle skidded to halt near Logan. "Get in!" Rafe yelled.

"No. Hayden's missing!" Logan shouted back. Hellish fires loomed around them. "Check the house. If that goes, the panic room might not withstand the heat."

Before they took two steps, another series of explosions shook the earth, decimating the last standing structure. *The ranch house.* A huge plume of fire hurled high into the sky.

Logan watched in horror as the house collapsed. His family was buried beneath the fire and rubble.

He shoved back all his emotions. He couldn't afford them. He ran toward the wall of flames. The devastating inferno burned like the fires of Hell itself.

Logan roared out orders for the men to get the bulldozers and fire equipment from the construction site and raze the house, clearing it away from the underground bunker. Those who survived the blast ran to start the desperate rescue. "You three," Logan shouted, "hunt for Hayden!"

"Rafe, call the fire department, and try to reach Zane." He scanned the destruction. Dear God, he couldn't lose them all.

"They'll get here as fast as they can!" Rafe yelled.

"What about the panic room?"

"Zane said as long as the generator has power they have air. It's hot, but they're okay for a while longer."

Logan's gut roiled. He turned to the men. "Get that house cleared, before it's too late."

Smoke burned Logan's eyes. "I need to find my son."

He took a bandana, covered his mouth and took off running. Rafe did the same. Logan caught sight of one of the large fire extinguishers brought from the construction site. Depending on where Hayden was, they might need it. He motioned to Rafe, who grabbed it.

Logan raced from one area to another, calling for his son and searching everywhere. Hayden had to be all right. Logan had promised Kat he'd protect them. Now they were all in danger.

The heat of the fire scorched his clothes as they kicked a path through burning debris. Hayden could be anywhere.

Despair clawed at Logan's gut. Methodically, frantically, they searched each pile of rubble, before rushing to the next one.

Finally, they reached the newly capped well. Only twenty feet west, the ranch was untouched by flame.

A strange tinny sound lifted over the clamor around them.

"What's that?" Rafe asked, turning in a circle, searching for the source of the noise.

Logan concentrated, trying to identify it. "A siren, but it doesn't sound right. More like a...." Realization hit. "Hayden's fire engine!"

They bolted toward the burning remains of the oldest barn on his property.

Tim, the young ranch hand, lay dead, his throat slit. Bloody footprints led toward the toy fire engine resting twenty feet beyond, its waning siren still going off.

Acid burned the back of Logan's throat as he tore through the area, fear licking through his veins. Each piece of wood he shifted, each step he took, he braced himself to find his son—injured or worse.

He'd killed men; men had died around him and Logan had never been more scared than when he peered behind the well to the last spot that seemed possible.

His knees buckled. Another body lay spread out, his head blown half off, a serrated Bowie knife by his hand. Tiny footprints marred the bloody soil next to him.

"Hayden!" Where was he? He followed the prints as they grew ever fainter, then froze as he saw tire tracks gouged into the surface of the earth as if a heavy vehicle had spun out on the dirt. Signs of blood and a skirmish led away from the ranch.

Hayden had been kidnapped.

LOGAN'S PHONE RANG, and he reached for it blindly, unable to look away from the evidence. "Carmichael."

"Hey, boss." His foreman's tired voice came over the line, along with the harsh sound of a siren. "Fire engine's here."

Logan cut him off. "And the panic room?"

Rafe raced to Logan's side. He hit the speakerphone. "What's happening there?"

"The ranch house burned like hellfire. We cleared what debris we could without exploding any of the gas tanks, or burning the men handling them—"

"How much longer?" Logan's gut churned with worry.

"The fire hose soaked the rest of the debris, so the entrance should be clear in ten minutes. Maybe less. It'll be dangerous, but..."

"Get it done." Logan swore. Adrenaline had his heart slamming out of his chest. "Ten minutes might be too long. We lost contact with Zane shortly after the blast. Hurry."

"Got it...and Sheriff Redmond and Deputy Parris are on their way. ETA five minutes. Dr. Sandoval called, but she's still a ways out."

"I'll be there in a minute."

Rafe had donned plastic gloves and he moved the arm on the dead body out of the way enough to expose what little remained of his face. "Think this is the guy who murdered Paulina?"

"I'd bet on it."

Logan studied the man. "Wait a minute. He looks familiar..." Logan tore the guy's shirt aside to reveal a dirty bandage on his shoulder. Logan ripped it off. Gun-shot wound to the shoulder. "This is the guy I shot. He locked Kat and me in the burning barn."

"Great. He's a psycho killer, and someone wanted *him* dead. Who the hell are we playing with here?"

"I don't know yet. ID?" Logan asked.

Rafe reached into the man's pocket and pulled out a driver's license. "Fake," he muttered. "But a good one. Hank Smith."

"Get his prints and we'll run the picture."

"If we don't hit, I'll call in some favors in D.C. and run it through Interpol."

Logan studied the ground around his ranch hand's body. "Tire tracks didn't come this far. Where's the second intruder?"

"He probably took Hayden," Rafe said quietly.

"Victor wants us dead. The king wants Kat and Hayden alive." Logan shot to his feet. "I don't know what happened here, but for now, let's get to the ranch house and help there."

They ran through the fiery chaos that used to be the Triple C ranch. Logan lurched to a stop when the ranch house came into view. The firemen held the hose firm as water gushed out, soaking the smoking lumber, but too many sections over the panic room still smoldered and burned. Including where the second—secret—vertical escape hatch should have been. He prayed the electronics there would still work. They had to get Kat and the others out.

Logan jumped onto an unused bulldozer. Once seated, he shoved the machine into gear and drove into the hellish, flaming debris. Fiery heat and steam blasted him. Overheated oxygen seared his lungs. The firemen turned the hose to drench him and the area around him. Over and over again, he smashed the bulldozer through the rubble until he'd cleared a path to the panic room's second escape hatch.

Logan turned off the bulldozer and jumped down. Water soaked him as he clawed in desperation at the wreckage blocking the entryway. They had to be okay. They just had to.

Rafe and a few others joined Logan and soon they cleared enough burned lumber, ash and dirt from the now-slick iron stairwell to reveal the safety door with its covered keypad. The metal was hot to the touch, but it appeared the insulation had protected the electrical panel inside from melting down. He prayed it still worked.

With shaking fingers, Logan hit the combination.

The door creaked open.

"Kat? Lanie?" Before he could finish, Kat burst through the door carrying their daughter.

"We're here, Logan." Kat threw herself into Logan's arms. "Hayden," she gasped. "Some men in a car took him away! We saw it." She clung to him, tears streaming down her face. "A black SUV. A man with a knife was going to kill Hayden. Another man shot the guy with the knife," she sobbed. "Then this car came out of nowhere. They grabbed Hayden and headed away from the house."

Logan looked at Zane. "You get a plate?"

He nodded. "One of the cars from the king's entourage. No ID on the shooter. Yet."

Logan's body went ice cold with fury. His son had almost died. The king had taken him. Someone would pay.

"I want Hayden," Lanie wailed. "I wanna go home."

Kat hugged her baby. "I know, sweetie. I know."

Logan's phone rang. When he recognized the king's number his jaw tightened. He pressed the speakerphone. "You've gone too far, Leopold. Where's my son?"

"I've gone too far!" the king roared. "My grandson would have died in your care. I saved him from those who would murder him."

"Where is he?" Kat yelled.

"Since you can't keep your children safe from danger, I'm bringing him to Bellevaux. Come to me and I will protect you."

"No!" Kat shouted. "He will never stay there. I will never stay there. I want my son!"

"He's in my custody now and under my protection," her father said in a cool voice. "I'm the king."

"You're mad," Kat yelled.

"Be that as it may, your son is alive because of my intervention, Katherine. Now, come take your proper place and I will protect you."

"You're his grandfather, how can you do this?"

"I will do anything to save my country," he said. "You don't understand, caught up in your little world, but it's important to my people—your people—that this country survive. I refuse to let them be swallowed up and our traditions lost."

Logan put his hand over the speaker. "Tell him what he wants to hear, Kat. Rafe and Zane will watch over Gretchen and Lanie. We're leaving now."

Kat froze, but realized she had no choice.

"All right. I'm coming. But he is my son. If he's hurt, you won't like my reaction."

"You may make a good queen, after all," the king mused. "I'll be waiting. Logan knows the way."

THE DUKE OF SARBONNE gazed at the tapestry lining the throne-room wall. The king hadn't entered the area since the explosion so the duke had commandeered the space. Leopold probably didn't even know. Weakling that he was. He faced his aide. "Niko, what news do you bring that has you trembling this time?"

The man stiffened. "King Leopold has made a surprisingly forceful move. He kidnapped his grandson."

"Really." The duke paced the marble floors. "I didn't think he had it in him." He turned on Niko. "Where is the boy now?"

"The young prince is on the way to Bellevaux via the king's private jet. He should be here within six hours. Our contact said the king has prepared two sets of adoption papers. One for the princess. One for the boy."

"He won't live that long." The duke sat on the jewel-encrusted throne and leaned back, tapping his index fingers together. "Plan an interception. The boy can't live. I *need* the princess. Only by joining our bloodlines together will I cement my hold on the throne."

"Your Grace," the man interjected. "May I point out that where the boy goes, the princess will follow?"

The duke smiled. "Kidnap him again, Niko? It's risky. I'll have to take out the king's entourage." He stared up at his inspiration—the tapestry of his ancestor's greatest victory. "Kill them all, but bring the boy to me."

This plan was worthy of the first Duke of Sarbonne. "The princess will hate her father for what he's done. I'll offer her an attractive alternative. She will become queen and I will become king on Christmas. Her child shall live." He fingered his whip. "For now…"

"You will control Bellevaux…and its new wealth with Victor Karofsky's contracts."

The duke's fingers drummed along the gold-plated arm of the throne. "Tell Victor Karofsky I am changing plans. We complete the transfer of power tonight. If he wants the mineral rights, he will make this all work."

"Y…Your Grace, Karofsky is a dangerous man—"

"And I am not?" the duke roared, slashing the man with his whip. "Who will rule Bellevaux. Me or Karofsky?"

The man clenched his fists and bowed low. "You, Your Grace."

The duke reveled in the blood running down Niko's face. "Don't forget again. We do this when *I* decide. I want duplicates of the adoption papers. As soon as the princess becomes the king's heir, I'll marry her."

"And King Leopold?"

The duke smiled, and fingered his bloodstained whip. "It's a shame how…accident prone…he's about to become."

He looked up at the tapestry. Soon. Roland, Duke of Sarbonne would restore the rightful bloodline and begin the next royal dynasty. King Roland and Queen Katherine of Bellevaux.

Their children would be strong and powerful. Never weak. Or they would be eliminated.

"Prepare the prison for a special set of visitors. As soon as the papers are signed, the king and the pretender prince will die."

Chapter Ten

Deke crouched in the hidden closet at the back of the king's jet, the one used to secret the monarch should his plane come under attack. Fear sent sweat trickling down Deke's back. He prayed no one checked in here or he was dead. He'd crawled to the farthest end of the space so no one opening the door would see him. But, if they glanced inside...

His entire body had gone numb in the cramped quarters, but nothing mattered except surviving, then saving Maria.

Victor Karofsky's network extended everywhere, and one of his henchmen had infiltrated the king's guards. Deke had used that contact to gain access to the plane. Now he remained concealed—actually trapped—within the enemy camp, but he'd had no other way to reach Bellevaux.

His face was probably plastered all over the internet and news stations by now. Hans's body would have been found. It wouldn't take long to make an ID through Interpol, and Deke had traveled with him. Deke's own identification may already have been made.

Footsteps approached the back of the plane. People stood outside the closet where Deke hid.

"Why are we in here? This is the king's bedroom."

"You have new orders, Sergei."

"What are you talking about?" the captain of the royal guard asked.

"You're going to die for your country."

A grunt, then a crash sounded against the wall right in front of Deke. Another muffled cry came from the main part of the plane, along with a child's screams.

"Drug the boy and help me hide these bodies."

The cries died away, and an ominous silence filtered into Deke's hiding place, then the door whipped open and the bodies of Sergei and another man were shoved into the closet. One corpse fell sideways on Deke, but he didn't dare move for fear of discovery.

"Call the duke."

After a moment, a voice said, "Your Grace. It is done. Those faithful to the king are dead. We have control of the plane. The boy is yours."

Stunned, Deke strained to hear beyond the wall. *Was this the start of a coup?* It was too soon. Victor had particular plans in place.

"I understand. The plane will be diverted, as requested, to the new location."

Another bit of silence.

"Thank *you,* Your Majesty! I, too, look forward to the new dawn of Bellevaux under your command."

Deke waited until the man left the luxurious bedroom and pulled out his satellite phone, weighing the risk of calling for help. But, Deke had run out of options. Victor would kill Maria. Swallowing the burning acid rising in his throat, he pressed a series of numbers then hit the call button. He had to have help.

"Maria?" A weak cough sounded. "Where have you been? I've been—"

"Pierre," Deke interrupted in a low whisper. "It's me."

The man let out a sound of disgust. "Why are you calling me, you piece of scum? Where is my daughter? I can't reach her." A fit of coughing on the phone dissolved into a groan of pain.

"What happened, Pierre? Are you all right?"

"I was careless. I crossed the duke and paid for it. The scars and bones will heal, but my hatred of him won't."

"I'm in trouble, Pierre. You were right about Victor. I failed my mission. He has Maria. I need your help."

Urgent whispering filtered in through the phone. Deke's body went ice cold. "Who's with you, Pierre?"

"I cannot say in case you are caught, but he may be able to help us. Tell me everything."

Trembling, Deke put the phone to his ear.

"The king's grandson and I are on the jet, returning to Bellevaux, but the duke's men have diverted the plane. Once we land, the boy is his and the child will be a pawn to ensure the duke becomes king."

"Sarbonne has planned a coup?"

"Against Victor's wishes. He wants the princess to solidify his position—according to what I heard."

Pierre sucked in a breath.

More whispers.

"If you can discover where the plane will land in time, we might be able to stop this."

"You know of a way to save Maria?"

"I have friends who can help…if you help them."

"Anything," Deke said, his eyes burning with emotion. "I'll do anything to keep Maria safe and take down Victor Karofsky."

LOGAN PACED THE PLANE, willing it to reach Bellevaux so they could rescue Hayden. He hated not being there. The news that the plane had been essentially hijacked and diverted enraged Logan. The king didn't want the boy dead. Logan didn't know what the duke had planned— only that he wanted the throne. And Kat.

"Why hasn't Noah called back?" asked Kat. "They must have found the plane by now."

"He and Hunter were tracking it down. We'll have word soon." But Logan feared the worst. All evidence indicated the duke was insane. A sadistic pretender intent on taking over the throne.

Logan sat across from Kat and reached for her hand. He couldn't believe the strength she showed in the past few hours. The grace under pressure. She might not want to be ruler of Bellevaux, but she certainly had the courage of a monarch.

The satellite phone sitting on the table between them rang. Kat stared at it, her face pinched and strained. Their gazes met, and, in her eyes, he saw mirrored the hope and fear that consumed them both.

He lifted the receiver.

She stopped him. "Don't hide anything from me."

He nodded. "No more secrets. No more lies."

Not between them. He pressed the speakerphone. "Carmichael."

"Falcon here. We didn't get to the airport in time." Noah Bradford's voice growled through the phone. "Everyone's dead, and Hayden's gone."

Kat cried out in distress and launched herself at Logan. He held her close.

"What happened?"

"A massacre. Sergei. The pilots. The royal guard. All dead. Some were killed in the plane. Others were gunned down on the tarmac."

"Oh, my God. Where's my baby?" Kat moaned. "We have to find him."

"We may have lucked out in that. We have an informant, one of the underground loyalists fighting to keep the monarchy. He went undercover at a prison where he heard rumors of torture and killings of political prisoners happening under the duke's command. The place is more like a dungeon. The man's been told to prepare for special guests."

"Hayden?" Aghast, Kat leaned toward the phone. "We have to save him. Is this man sure?"

"Is he reliable?" Logan added.

"I'd say yes to both counts. The man isn't young, but brave and determined to take down the duke. Pierre was caught confirming Daniel's existence in the prison and beaten badly."

Logan let out a sigh of relief. He hugged Kat closer.

"Daniel's alive?"

"Barely…but he knows we're coming," added Noah. "He's been tortured for months. Severely. He's so broken, he may not be able to walk again."

Logan forced himself to remain calm as dangerous emotions clawed to the surface. "Why is the duke doing this?"

"Evidently he can trace his lineage back to some thug in the middle ages who ruled Bellevaux. A *Marquis de Sade* type who was eventually beheaded by his loyal subjects. Sarbonne feels that he should rightly be king."

"Sarbonne doesn't have that kind of power. How can he think this will succeed?"

"According to Sierra, the duke came into a lot of money recently. We're talking hundreds of millions of dollars. It was well hidden, but my sister tracked it down. She's still searching for the original source of the money."

Logan sat back in his chair. "Could the duke have

been Stefan's leak? Could he have set up the bombing at the royal court?"

"The timing of some of the deposits coincide. I'd say the duke plans to try to bring back his glory days—with a little help from the black market and Victor Karofsky. The same one whose gun-running empire you disrupted while with the CIA."

A warning beacon sounded over the speakerphone. The pilot's voice squawked through the intercom.

"Mr. Carmichael. We're being ordered to land by the Bellevaux Air Force. They're directing us to a private airport."

Logan pressed the intercom. "Give me the coordinates and ETA, then do as they say."

"Yes, sir."

"You heard?" Logan asked Noah.

"Be very careful. We don't know the duke's plans, but the man's insane."

"Arrange a rescue operation for the prison," Logan ordered, looking over at Kat. "I have a feeling when the duke talked about special guests, he was also talking about us."

THE PLANE LANDED and started its final taxi. A phalanx of cars sat at the end of the runway, their presence ominous.

Kat shuddered, fear for her son and Logan paralyzed her. "The duke could kill you. Hayden, too." The words choked out as a sob.

Logan held her hands in his. "He can try."

"What can we do?"

"Stay alive. Whatever it takes. Lying. Kowtowing to the egotistical bastard. Make him believe that he's succeeding until Noah and Hunter can get to us."

"I'm afraid," she whispered, seeing the determined warrior in Logan's expression.

"You're right to be afraid, but try not to let it show. You're a princess, Kat. From the intel, the duke seems to see you as a future ruler alongside him. Act the part. Do whatever you must to survive. Our children need you to live."

Was Logan saying that he didn't expect to?

He squeezed her hands and held her gaze captive. "No matter what happens, Kat. Promise me you will not antagonize Sarbonne. You must live to protect our son."

The words answered everything, and she knew Logan was saying goodbye, just in case.

She couldn't lose him. She'd been such a fool not to trust him for so long. He'd shown in every way how he would fight for her and the children. How he would use his strength—and his wealth—to ensure the safety of others. She'd been unable to see past her fear that he was a man of integrity, of courage. He was a hero, something she'd never believed in before.

The plane rolled to a stop, and they rose from their seats.

With a cry, Kat wrapped her arms around his waist, holding him tight. She rested her head against his strong chest, taking comfort in the heat of his body and the solid rhythm of the strong beat of his heart. "There's so much we haven't talked about…what I said last night—"

"Kat, you don't have to explain."

Reluctantly, she pulled away and pressed her fingers to his lips. "Yes, I do. Growing up, I was taught that I shouldn't believe in anything or anyone. That I could only count on myself, but from the moment we met, I believed in you. You were my knight in shining armor from the beginning, and that scared me. I'm sorry I wasted so much time. You've made my dreams come true," she whispered. "I couldn't have asked for a better man to be the father of my children."

"And I couldn't have asked for a braver mother. Say whatever you have to. Do whatever you have to. But don't give up."

The airlock hissed and the outer hatch opened. Armed men boarded the plane.

They grabbed Logan and pushed him toward the door. He looked back at Kat. "Stay alive."

Her eyes glistened. Another guard gripped her arm and shoved her forward.

Kat followed Logan down the steps. He stood close to her side. A limousine flying Bellevaux's flag pulled up to them.

A striking man exited the vehicle, tall, dark-haired, his uniform decorated with too many medals to count. Kat's gaze dropped to the whip in his hand.

"Princess. Mr. Carmichael."

"Your Grace," Logan said, his voice tight, but Kat remained silent.

The duke frowned at her. "No pleasantries? Well, I suppose this isn't the most pleasant of circumstances, is it?" He turned to Logan. "Especially for you, Carmichael."

Kat glanced back and forth between the two men. A palpable hatred resonated. How well did Logan know the man who held her son?

He stepped in front of Katherine. "I am the Duke of Sarbonne, Princess Katherine." He bowed with a flourish, then kissed her hand. "It is a pleasure to meet you."

She tried to shake off his hand, but he held tight. Painfully so.

"You are coming with me," he said softly, then gestured to Logan. "He remains here."

"No." Logan shoved the duke aside, breaking his hold on Kat.

Two guards grabbed Logan's arms and shoved them behind his back. He didn't flinch.

"Do you wish to die here and now?" Sarbonne roared, brushing at the spot on his jacket where Logan had pushed him. "No one touches a member of the royal family and lives."

"You're not a member of the royal family. You're a psycho," Logan taunted. "Always have been. You're the descendant of a by-blow pretender and a bully who killed his own brother to take the throne."

"And you are my sacrificial lamb. You and Stefan wreaked havoc on my partner's businesses and he wants revenge. My financial benefactor will be squarely in my corner when I deliver you to him."

Kat cried out in protest.

"Shut up, woman. I have the blood of kings in my veins," the duke said. "With you by my side and the treasury overflowing, nothing will stop Bellevaux from becoming great again. You will do as I say or die, as well." Sarbonne turned to his guards. "Take him. I want Logan Carmichael to understand the power I have over him."

The guards shoved Logan to the ground, kicking him and punching him, until he couldn't stop a groan from escaping. In triumph, the duke watched as blood spattered on the asphalt.

Kat ran to Logan. "Stop. You're killing him."

Logan met her gaze, willing her to be silent, then curled up defensively as the largest guard grabbed him by the hair and the other repeatedly slugged his face and body.

Kat threw herself between Logan and the guards, and one man accidentally belted her across the jaw.

Her head popped back and she let out a cry, falling to the tarmac.

"That's my future wife, you imbecile," the duke yelled. He beat the guard across the face, leaving raw strips of flesh bleeding from the lash.

The guard sank to his knees, and the duke yanked Kat to her feet.

"You live only as long as you remain a true and faithful wife, Princess. Remember that."

She clenched her fists and bit her tongue.

"Kat," Logan said, his gaze intent with meaning. "Think of our son."

The duke's turned red and faced Logan. "Your son? You're the bastard who sullied my future queen?"

With a shout, the duke grabbed the automatic weapon from the adjacent guard's hand, fired, holding the trigger back. Bullets strafed Logan and everyone near him, cutting them down in a bloody mess.

No!" Kat dove toward the duke, grappling for the gun.

He smashed it off her head, and she collapsed at his feet.

He bent down and gripped her hair hard, yanking her face near his. "Look at your hero now." He forced her head in the direction of the pile of bodies. Blood splattered the corpses. "I mean what I say, Princess. You will have no one but me, or *everyone* you love will die. Starting with your precious son."

SITUATED ABOVE THE AIRPORT, Deke couldn't believe what he'd seen.

Logan Carmichael. Dead.

The man Deke knew only as the Falcon stood beside

him. No emotion showed on the man's face. He was cold, deadly looking, and Deke feared him almost as much as Karofsky.

Deke's mind whirled. What did this massacre mean for him? "Will you still help me now that Carmichael is dead?"

The Falcon turned to him and glared, then slipped his phone to his ear. "Plans have changed," he said in a low, deadly tone. "Carmichael just took six bullets to the chest. We move without him."

He clicked off and stared at Deke—the man's dark, dead eyes the most frightening Deke had ever seen.

"Betray me. Even think about it," the Falcon warned, "and you'll share a similar fate to them."

Deke looked down at the pile of dead bodies and shuddered, then followed in the Falcon's wake.

KAT COULDN'T BREATHE. Fear and horror filled her. Logan was dead.

She struggled against the remaining guards, wanting to run to Logan and touch him one last time. Grief crippled her.

The duke turned on his heel and stalked to the limousine. "Bring the princess. She has some papers to sign before we wed."

Hysteria threatened, but Kat closed her eyes, willing herself not to scream at the agony in her heart. Tears streamed down her face. She didn't care if the monster waiting saw them, but Logan had warned her not to antagonize the duke. Logan wanted her to save their son, and she would, if she had to kill Sarbonne herself.

Kat remembered Logan's words. *Do anything. Say anything.* She took a deep breath and walked toward the maniac in his limousine, wiping her face as she went.

Just before she reached him, the duke closed the car door, then rolled down the window. "I don't think so. You have a lesson to learn first."

He signaled the guards. "Handcuff her and bring her to the prison. Let her have a taste of what she'll face if she doesn't learn to obey."

A guard slapped the metal restraints on her and pushed her into a filthy, white-panel van with no rear windows. The back section had been stripped down to bare metal, and the inside reeked of vomit, sweat, blood, urine…and death.

Kat gagged, but somehow maintained control. Logan's face and words gave her strength. He hadn't backed down in the face of the duke's insanity. Neither would she.

Every part of her ached, and her heart had shattered. How would she live without Logan?

"Where are you taking me?" Kat asked, praying the guard who sat across from where she lay bound would answer.

"Somewhere you won't come out of alive, unless you cooperate."

Kat stared at the guard's ravaged face. Maybe the lashing he'd just taken at Sarbonne's hands would make the man willing to defy the duke. "Will you help me escape?" she whispered.

The guard shook his head. "No. To cross the duke means punishment or even death. He has threatened my family." He leaned closer. "Give him what he wants. There's no other way to survive his gaol. Even if you do, you won't come out of his prison as pretty as you are going in. The duke revels in inflicting pain."

"Shut up, Antoine," the driver hissed. "He's probably listening."

Kat shivered. The duke wanted her as his queen. She would have to find a way to use the fact to her advantage.

"Is the king part of this?" she asked. "Does he know the duke is killing people?"

"Leopold has grown soft, and won't be king much longer. He has named no legal heir and the country is in turmoil. You'd better learn quickly who has the power," Antoine said. "With you under the duke's control, no one can help our country now."

Kat stared at him. "Why are you telling me this?"

Antoine put a hand against the whip marks on his cheek. "Because you were our country's last hope."

Kat froze. Was he saying that he *wanted* her to be queen? That he actually hoped she would come to Bellevaux and become the king's heir?

Antoine glanced toward the front, then whispered one last time, "The duke intends to kill you after you're married. If you can get away, *run*—and don't ever come back."

THE VEHICLE EASED through a large gate with a half-dozen guards standing by with machine guns. Once security waved them through, Kat's heart plummeted at the distance from the fence to their destination. How could she possibly get Hayden away without being caught?

The car came to a stop outside an old stone building that looked like something from a medieval horror movie. The duke's prison. Her heart raced when Antoine helped her out of the back. Her manacled wrists made it difficult to exit on her own.

He used more gentle hands. "I'll pray for you, Princess. I'm sorry."

A group of guards forced Kat down stone steps toward a large iron door. It took two guards to open it.

The door clanged shut behind their entourage, sounding much like a death knell. The stone-lined corridor closed in on her. They passed a series of rooms, the furniture within old and tattered. The farther underground they walked, the more Kat's hope dimmed. Finally they reached a locked iron door.

The gate eased open. An older man struggled, wincing as he pressed the hefty iron weight back. The slashes across his face and neck looked remarkably familiar. Whip marks. Another of the duke's victims. She wanted to beg for help, but he didn't meet her gaze.

"End of the hall," a guard said, pushing her roughly. "Don't talk to anyone."

Kat walked down the stone hallway, her gaze shifting right, then left. They'd entered the prison now, and the dungeon chilled her. Not because of the cool temperature, but the horror she witnessed. Blood marked the floors and even the walls of several cells. Sharp metal objects rested on surgical tables. Sharp...and stained dark from use.

This was not just a prison. It was the duke's torture chamber.

Kat wanted to escape, but her son could be at the end of this hall. Part of her wanted him to be there, so she could see he was okay. Another part of her wanted him never to have seen anything like this horror in his lifetime. She would kill the duke for doing this to her son.

Halfway down the corridor, a groan penetrated her numbed mind. A man—or what was left of one—lay on the floor of one of the prison cells on her right. He gazed at her from a bruised and battered face, raising his chin proudly.

She paused, staring into his eyes. He seemed to will her his strength. Did he know who she was? Could this be Daniel? The man that Logan had talked about being imprisoned and tortured? His face, although badly beaten, reminded her of Logan's—the warrior's expression, the obvious determination to survive, to fight.

Kat nodded to him, and turned away. She would survive this, too. No matter what the duke did. She would summon her courage to withstand the torture. She would lie, cheat and steal to save herself and the life of her son. Then she would wait for the time she could have her revenge.

The guard pushed her forward and opened a locked door at the end of a hallway.

Kat walked into the filthy stone room. A soiled mat lay on the floor and Hayden sat in a chair next to the duke, her son's dirty face streaked with tears.

"Mommy!" He ran to her and Kat looped her handcuffed hands around him and held him close. A protective anger, stronger than any emotion she'd ever felt in her life, besides grief, swept through her.

"I don't like it here, Mommy." His words were slightly slurred. "I want to go back to Daddy's house."

"Shhh, baby," she whispered. "I'm here." They'd drugged him. A little boy.

She scanned the room, refusing to let the revulsion and fear show on her face. The wooden table before her was stained with blood. Cuffs, whips and more metal instruments lay ready for use.

The duke leaned back, completely comfortable in the disturbing surroundings.

"Why did you bring Hayden here? This is no place for a child."

"The boy?" the duke asked, expansively. "Why, this is his new home."

Kat stilled, staring around in shock. "You're making him stay here?"

"I see I finally have your attention, my dear." The duke flicked an imaginary piece of lint from his crisp pants.

"Yes, Princess Katherine. He stays here." He leaned forward, his eyes cold, yet triumphant. "Now, this is the plan. You will accompany me to the palace. You will sign the adoption papers to become the king's heir. Then you will marry me immediately. When I claim the throne, you will rule by my side as my queen, or you will disappear."

"But my son—"

"Remains here as collateral."

At her attempted protest, the duke slashed his whip off the wall. "The next lash is for him."

Kat froze in place, her arms around a terrified Hayden.

"Understand this, Princess. There is *no* negotiation. If you do not do as I say, your son dies. Your daughter follows once I find her." The duke rose. "And make no mistake, I will find her."

Kat hugged Hayden closer. "Please don't make him stay here."

"Would you prefer I kill him now? That's his other option."

She felt the blood drain from her face. She swayed, ready to break, then, with monumental effort, pulled herself together.

She couldn't fall apart. She had to be strong. Do whatever it took to survive. The guard had been sympathetic. She would find other allies in Bellevaux. She would get Hayden out of here. Her son would not die.

The duke stared at her. "You're too quiet. Whatever desperate plot you're concocting, forget it. It won't work."

"I just want to be near my son."

The duke's eyes gleamed. "Not until you've done as I command."

"Can't he stay somewhere in the palace? Away from everyone?" Kat forced herself to walk across the room and look at the monster with pleading eyes. "Please."

"No. You will have other children living there. Legitimate children. *My children.*"

"O-of course." Kat forced herself not to gag at the idea of letting this man touch her. She focused on Logan's instructions. *Say anything.* "But I need to know if I do what you say, Hayden will be safe. Since we are to be married, I want to trust you."

The duke's face softened a bit. "You are a fighter, like a mother bear…and you're very beautiful. Those are two traits befitting a queen." He touched her cheek. "Never let it be said I don't listen to reason. Once we are married, we'll talk again."

He smiled when he said it, but Katherine knew better. Hayden wouldn't ever be free of this prison. He would be used to keep her in line, and at the duke's mercy.

Her future husband opened the door and called in the old guard. "Pierre."

The duke held out his hand. "You will come with me now, Katherine. I have someone I wish you to meet."

Hayden clung to her. Kat knelt down and kissed his hair. "Mommy will be back. I promise."

"If you behave," the duke said, "that may be the truth." He turned to the old guard. "Take the boy from her."

Pierre stood in front of Kat and Hayden. As he did so, he slipped a small metal shiv into her palm. Her gaze flashed to his face, but the man kept his eyes lowered. Kat's heart pounded as she bent her wrist to ease the blade beneath the shirtsleeve cuff. She prayed it wouldn't slip out onto the floor. The man's life would be forfeit.

Pierre stepped aside so she could pass, and he held Hayden's shoulders firmly. Tears rolled down her son's cheeks, and Kat fought against the burning behind her eyes. She glanced back. The guard whispered in Hayden's ear and her son nodded. He waved at Kat and she swallowed deeply. *How could she leave him here?*

She met the duke's cruel gaze. *How could she not?*

Unless…she let the knife edge into her palm.

A groan sounded. Kat paused and peered into a cell. A pile of rags in the corner moved. Oh, my God. It was a man.

"Unlock this door," the duke said to Antoine.

He fit the key in and pulled open the iron. Sarbonne led her inside, but stayed near the entrance.

"This piece of trash has now outlived his usefulness." The duke stopped. "Except for an introduction and a warning." The duke tapped his whip against his hand. "Don't worry. He's chained and too broken to give us any problems."

The pitiful being stirred again, forcing himself to move. His hair looked dark, but then Kat recognized the filth and blood caked in his hair and realized he was a blond. Ice-blue eyes stared back at her, and her heart started beating wildly in her chest.

He had her eyes. It couldn't be.

He lifted his swollen chin. They'd broken his nose, and maybe his cheekbones, but obviously not his spirit. Admiration, coupled with horror, welled within her.

Kat heard a noise in the doorway, and glanced behind her. Both Antoine's and Pierre's eyes were full of pity.

The duke circled the man, whip in hand, but kept at a distance. "This, my dear Katherine, is what is left of mighty Prince Stefan of Bellevaux. Your half brother."

"Oh, my God," she whispered.

"The world believes he's dead," the duke said, laying a lash across Stefan's back. "They'll soon be right."

Stefan grasped the bars to his left and struggled to stand himself upright on one leg. Kat stared in disbelief at the signs of brutality and viciousness his body bore.

"Remember this day, Katherine. Stefan disappointed me. I don't deal well with disappointment." He sent the whip cracking across her brother's chest and laughed at Kat's cry of distress.

Fury swept through her. Sarbonne was showing her what was to be her fate, and that of her son. It would not come to pass.

Kat met her half brother's gaze and held her hand off to the side, revealing the tip of the knife in her sleeve. His eyes widened and then she saw a smile upturn his lips.

"You think this is funny?" the duke roared in anger, lashing him again.

"No," Stefan whispered, his voice husky. "I think you're funny, Roland. I think you're a joke."

The duke's face turned red. Kat paled until she realized what her brother was doing. Risking his life to distract the duke, waiting for her to kill him. With a silent prayer, she let the knife fall into her hands. Terrified, she raised her fist, ready to stab the duke.

A gasp from the hallway had the duke whirling to face her. He blocked her strike with his whip, then backhanded her across the room. The knife slid across the floor.

"I warned you." The duke unfurled the whip in his hands. "You will not disobey me again."

The lash came down, stinging across her arm, and she cried out at the pain. Antoine shoved Sarbonne away. He fell back on the ground and before he could rise, Stefan tackled him.

Kat watched in disbelief as her brother grabbed the duke by the throat, and with one motion, encircled the leather lash around Sarbonne's neck and pulled tight.

"No!" The duke clawed at Stefan's hold, kicking and fighting to be free. His hand found the knife and he started to swing.

One second later, he was dead.

Chapter Eleven

Stefan rolled over on his back, breathing hard. The duke's lifeless body lay on the floor beside him. Pierre and Antoine, the guard who had helped them, stood in the doorway.

Shocked and relieved, Kat lay curled on the dirty stones, her body still aching from the lash. She met Stefan's pain-filled gaze.

"The guards may still kill us," her brother warned.

"No, they won't," Pierre said. "They will be either rejoicing or running. The king will not let this attempted coup pass unpunished."

"Thank you," Kat said to Antoine as he helped her up. "You risked a lot for me. You saved my life."

Fading fear and restored dignity shone in the battered guard's eyes. "Will you and the prince now save our country? The duke did not work alone."

Kat faltered, then looked at her brother. He stared back at her, in silent inquiry, then when she hesitated, he closed his eyes and lay there on the stones, quiet.

"I will do what I can to help," she answered, then turned to Pierre. "Let my son out. Let all of the duke's prisoners out."

He bowed to her, with obvious deference. "Yes, Princess Katherine."

She stared after him as the guards hurried to open the other man's cell, stunned at the way they were acting toward her.

"Will you be all right, Stefan? I must get my son."

"Go to him," he said with a sad smile. "I'm not going anywhere…not under my own power at least."

Kat ran to Hayden's cell.

Pierre came closer, supporting a battered, bleeding man who introduced himself as Logan's partner, Daniel. His horrific bruises and wounds did little to quell his determination to stand erect, but Kat didn't know how the man did it. Every part of his body had been slashed or beaten.

"I can see why Logan couldn't get over you," Daniel said through cracked lips. "Will he be here soon?"

Her eyes filled with tears. "Logan is dead. The duke…" she choked out, barely able to say the words. It made them real.

The light went out in Daniel's eyes, his joy replaced with a cold anger. "Then it's a good thing the duke is already dead."

Pierre unlocked Hayden's cell, and the old guard now stood back, smiling and tugging the heavy door with him.

The iron squeaked open. Hayden stood in the doorway, terrified, looking around her at the large men by her side. "Mommy?" he whispered, obviously wanting to run to her, but afraid to leave the room.

"The bad man's gone, sweetie. You're safe." Kat's heart broke at the cautious expression on her precious son's face, but she could see when her words finally hit home.

His face lit up with joy, and his fear left him.

He bolted toward her, arms outstretched. "Mommy!"

She swept him into her arms and hugged him close, rocking to and fro. She couldn't stop the tears from flowing freely. Tears of joy for what she had. Tears of sorrow for the man she'd lost. "Look at your poor little face," she said, touching the bruise on his cheek.

"Don't cry, Mommy." Hayden patted her. "Owies go away." He looked over her shoulder expectantly. "Where's Daddy?"

Grief nearly overwhelmed her, but she managed a smile. "Daddy can't be here. Something happened—"

The main entrance to the prison door slammed open. Several men burst into the room, weapons drawn. Kat whirled around and moved in front of Hayden, protecting him from view. Two other guards turned their automatic weapons toward Kat and her son. Pierre and Antoine stepped in front of them, their guns drawn, as Daniel reached her side and pushed her behind him.

Stefan stirred in his cell, but didn't move from where he lay, bent and broken on the floor. Kat's heart pounded in her chest. Who were these men? Daniel stood away from the stone wall, eyes hard as he waited. Kat felt him sway slightly and recognized in his trembling, the monumental effort it took for him to remain erect.

The king and another man entered and stood just inside the doorway to the dungeon. The armed bodyguards fanned out around them.

King Leopold stood, his face pale with shock, as he took in the lifeless body of the duke, then the bruised and bleeding ones of Kat, Hayden, the guards and finally Daniel.

Leopold's eyes widened in shock, then dismay. "Victor, my friend," the king said to the tall man at his side. "I'm sorry I didn't believe you."

Beside Kat, Pierre stiffened, anger flashing in his

eyes and his knuckles whitening against the grip of his gun. Even as he stared with hatred at Victor Karofsky, Pierre reached into his pocket and pressed what looked like a pager.

What was he doing? Was he signaling for help?

Victor put his hand on the king's shoulder. "I regret that I'm the one who had to tell you of the duke's treachery, Your Majesty. I know you trusted Sarbonne." Victor directed his bodyguards to step forward and gestured around him. "My men will take care of this mess for you and see the princess and her son safely back to the palace."

Kat clutched Hayden to her. The men around her closed ranks. "We are not going with him."

Pierre, Antoine and Daniel moved in closer, as did the few individuals remaining from the prison crew.

"Guards, stand down," the king ordered the men at Kat's side.

They didn't respond, merely held their guns trained on Victor.

Kat shifted from one foot to the other, surprised. She hadn't expected their loyalty.

The king's face turned red. "I ordered you to stand down. *I am your king.*"

"Their loyalty lies elsewhere, Father," Stefan said. "As should yours." He struggled to a seated position, the effort obviously causing pain.

"Stefan?" the king's voice trembled, his shock evident as he made his way toward his son. "It's not possible. The duke told me he found your body."

"He did. He found me unconscious and half dead, then brought me here to finish the job." Stefan tried to sit up farther and clenched his teeth so as not to cry out.

For the first time Kat recognized the man behind the king. A father who'd found his son.

Leopold knelt by his badly beaten son. "How did this happen?"

"Ask your friend, Victor. It was his hit. He was working with Sarbonne all the time."

Leopold spun around. Victor held his gun on the monarch, then signaled the bodyguards to grab the king.

"What is the meaning of this?" Leopold demanded.

Kat clutched Hayden's head to her chest and held her breath. Victor's men appeared ruthless. Would they get out of this horrible place alive? She glanced at Pierre, the man's face stone-still and unafraid. Were Logan's men still out there? She trusted him…. She had to believe in his plan—even if he was no longer leading.

"Who do you think backed Sarbonne's coup, Father?" Stefan said, bitterly. "Your *friend* is an arms dealer. The rare earth metals discovered in Bellevaux feed the manufacture of high-tech weaponry. Victor wanted those rights all along. He didn't care who gave them to him. You or the duke. Isn't that right, Karofsky? Anyone who opposed you disappeared or died, like my brother, Maximillian."

The king roared in fury, tugging against the guards who held him "*You* killed my son?"

"It doesn't matter now. Sign the papers you brought."

"Never."

"You have more than one child who can die here today, Leopold," Victor warned. "Don't be a fool."

"Were you behind the court massacre?"

"Stefan had to be eliminated."

"How'd that work out for you?" the prince taunted. "I'd ask for a refund from your hitman, if I were you. He missed."

"I won't," Victor said, turning the gun on Stefan.

"Logan and I destroyed you once, Karofsky. We'll do it again."

"Logan Carmichael is dead," Victor shot back. "The only positive thing the duke accomplished. And you're a useless cripple now."

"Tell that to Sarbonne," Stefan said defiantly. "He would disagree…if he could."

"I disagree, too." Logan stepped out from a secret entrance at the back of the dungeon. "Put down your weapons or die now, Karofsky."

Logan! Kat swayed. She couldn't believe it. Alive! His clothes torn and bloody, but the dark black of a Kevlar vest showed through his shirt. Joy like she'd never known swept through her.

She wanted to run to him, but he met her gaze and shook his head. *Soon*, he mouthed. *I love you.*

Several other men in black and camouflaged clothes came up behind Karofsky's men. They jammed guns to their heads. "Put them down. Now!"

Kat recognized Hunter's voice and realized the big man beside him must be Noah.

A third man on the landing held his weapon trained on Victor, hatred in his eyes.

"I would suggest you not hesitate," Logan said, his voice cold and deadly.

Kat drank in the sight of him as his tall, strong figure took command. Her head roared with joy. Alive. She hugged Hayden tight. Her heart beat again.

The bodyguards didn't fight. They placed their weapons on the floor and hit their knees.

"Cowards," Victor cursed, holding his gun on the king. "Deke." Victor nodded toward the man with Hunter and Noah. "This is not the way for your wife to survive. Assist me, and you will be rewarded. She will go free."

"I've heard your promises before, Victor. You're a liar. You deal with the devil to get what you want. Now you will pay. You won't leave this prison alive. I swear it."

Logan nodded at the restrained guards then eased his way toward Kat, each movement calculated, searching for an angle of attack. Kat held her breath. Hayden squirmed in her arms as Logan moved closer. Suddenly, he broke free and bolted toward Logan.

"Daddy!"

His happy greeting ended in a terrified cry as the arms dealer grabbed Hayden and held him to his chest, gun pressed under his chin.

"Mommy!"

Kat's heart sank. "Hayden."

Victor turned on Logan "Move, Carmichael. Even breathe in my direction and your son is dead. That goes for all of you. Now *you* put your weapons down."

Logan froze. Kat didn't dare look at him. Her eyes locked on to her son.

One of the former guards shifted. Victor fired off several rounds, killing two of the men. *"I said guns down. Now!"*

Hayden kicked and screamed in Victor's arms, terrified by the gunfire so close.

"Don't hurt him!" Kat shouted.

"Stop it!" Victor roared at the hysterical child. "The boy and I are leaving. The king comes with me to sign those papers." He jammed his gun harder into Hayden's throat. "Follow, and he dies."

"Hot! Hot!" Hayden screamed.

Kat reached out a hand.

Victor turned his gun on her. "Don't anyone else move."

Logan flashed a glance at Daniel, who stood closest to the terrorist, and made a subtle hand sign.

"Be ready, Princess," Daniel whispered in her ear.

"For what?"

"To duck."

With that, he and Logan launched themselves at Victor, taking him down and yanking his gun arm away from Hayden. Bullets sprayed the ceiling and ricocheted off the floor.

Hayden was thrown free. Kat ran to him and grabbed him close, huddling protectively around her son.

Logan tugged Victor to his feet and the arms dealer stared around the room in furious disbelief. It was over.

"I will hunt you down, Carmichael," he swore at Logan. "You'll pay for killing *my* son."

Deke flew across the room and shoved a shiv in Karofsky's stomach. "No. You will not harm anyone again."

Victor looked in shock at the metal shaft sticking from his body. Blood pumped steadily from the fatal wound.

"That was for Maria," Deke ground out. "And my unborn child."

"You will never find her now," Victor spat, sagging to his knees.

Deke stood over him, glaring down at the dying man. "I already have."

Pierre moved to Deke's side, and Logan left the arms dealer under their final watch. He raced to Kat.

"Are you and Hayden all right?" He kissed her face, then yanked her against him, careful not to crush their traumatized son in between.

"I thought I'd lost you," she said crying, touching Logan in disbelief. "I thought Sarbonne killed you."

Logan held her tight, cradling both her and Hayden in his powerful arms. "I told you he could try. Turns out I'm not that easy to kill." He looked at her, a sheen of moisture in his eyes, and gently pushed the hair back from her cheek. "Especially when I have something this precious to live for."

"I love you," Kat whispered, then sagged against his chest, listening to him murmur that he loved her, too, and everything would be all right. She closed her eyes against her own heartfelt tears, and gave thanks that they'd all survived.

"Call a medevac. Quick!"

Everyone turned at Stefan's shout. The king lay over his son, blood pouring from a bullet wound in his chest. Agony contorted his features.

"No," Kat cried, realizing Leopold had been shot trying to protect Stefan.

Logan ran to the king, and pressed his hands against the wound. Blood continued to seep through his fingers. "I need a pressure bandage."

Pierre stripped off his guard's jacket and pushed it into Logan's hands "Use this."

Kat came closer, holding Hayden's face protectively against her so he couldn't see the wound in his grandfather's chest. Her son had been through enough.

Logan's men and Antoine locked the remaining guards into a cell. Soon the hallway cleared.

"Father?" Kat said hesitantly, seeing the disturbing amount of blood he'd lost. Logan's ministrations seemed to stanch the wound, but the king's skin was mottled gray.

Leopold rolled his head to one side to look at her. "I'm sorry, Katherine. I never meant for things to go this far."

"Why did you risk this?"

Sorrow filled his eyes. "I know you don't understand, but I had to save my country. For that, I needed an heir."

"Father, what were you thinking?" Stefan said. "Bellevaux could have survived economically without getting involved with the likes of Victor Karofsky."

"I didn't understand what he was like. I was desperate. I did it for the love for my country."

Pierre cleared his throat. "I love Bellevaux, too, Your Majesty. But what you have done...it's wrong. Many good men have died because of you." He bowed to his sovereign one last time. "I can no longer, in good conscience, serve you as my king."

Leopold's face paled. Kat stared at the man who had taken her baby from her and tried to feel pity. She didn't know if she could ever forgive him. She'd almost lost both her children—and Logan—because of his schemes.

She clasped Logan's hand and kissed Hayden's temple, grateful they were both alive.

"Mommy, I want to go home." Hayden clung to Kat, his residual fear evident.

"We will, sweetie," she said, wondering exactly where that was now.

"You can't leave," Pierre blurted out in desperation. "You must take over as queen. Your country needs you."

Kat shook her head. "No, Pierre, my family needs me more. I don't want this. Stefan is alive. He can take his rightful place as the king's heir again."

"Pierre is right. The prince can't agree," Logan said.

"It's true," Stefan said weakly. "He knows the reasons I cannot be king, Father."

Leopold sank back. "Please don't abandon your country, Stefan. *I* will leave, if that's what you want. Live in exile, never to return. I know what I've done is unforgivable."

Kat stared at her father, sadness and respect rising within her.

"You saved my life," Stefan whispered, the effort to speak resonating in his voice.

"But—"

"It's not your transgressions that prevent me from being king."

"I don't understand."

"Explain to my father," Stefan requested of Logan, then fell back, exhausted.

Logan held Kat close and looked at Leopold. "Your son sacrificed more than anyone could expect. His political junkets as Prince Stefan enabled him to get access to information and make contacts that were critical to the fight on terrorism."

"What?" The king turned on his son. "You never told me. How dare you risk your life. You are royalty."

"Maximillian was heir. Before his death. I wanted to do something with mine besides be a playboy prince."

Her brother reminded Kat so much of Logan.

"We discovered the duke leaked Stefan's identity to Karofsky," Logan said. "He wanted Stefan dead. Right before the explosion at the royal court, his name appeared on a series of hit lists revealing his work with Interpol and the CIA. The wrong people know about his double life."

"No," Kat whispered, recognizing the implications.

Stefan gave Kat a regretful glance. "I'm dead now… to the world and to those terrorists. If I don't remain that way," Stefan said quietly, "my murder won't be merely a ruse. It will be a reality and everyone around me will be at risk."

"But I can't lose you again, Stefan," the king insisted. "Not a second time."

"After today, Stefan will no longer exist. My face has been shattered irrevocably. My body, too. When I am put back together, I'll become someone new, and dedicate my life, in whatever capacity my recovery will allow, to stopping men like Sarbonne and Karofsky."

"Then you have decided," the king said sadly. "Bellevaux is lost."

MEDICS STABILIZED DANIEL for his ride to the palace, where a hospital room was being set up. Noah and Hunter supervised the impending transport of a badly injured man known to the ambulance crew only as Léon—his destination would remain unknown.

Kat clutched her brother's hand, hating that she would probably never see him again. "I wish I could have gotten to know you," she said. She leaned down, her mouth just inches from his ear. "My children will miss having an uncle," she whispered, "and I, an amazing brother."

Léon kissed her cheek. "I think we would have been good friends. Not just siblings. Your courage in the prison saved me. Good luck, *ma soeur*. Be safe."

The stretchers rolled out. The king's stretcher was placed in the last ambulance and as his son's vehicle left, Leopold watched, then bowed his head, a broken, sorrowful man.

Logan couldn't believe the change in the king in the past hour. The once proud man had grown small and old, his weakened body trembling as he lay bereft on the gurney.

"What are you going to do?" Pierre asked, his face stoic.

The king lifted his head, his eyes dark with anguish. "What I must," Leopold said. "I caused one son's death, another son's unspeakable torture and now his…loss… forever from my life. I kidnapped my own grandchild. I do not deserve to be king."

He turned his face away. "I must prepare our people to no longer have a country to call their own."

"No," Pierre objected. "If you do not name an heir, our country will cease to exist."

"Perhaps that's for the best," Leopold said, and turned away.

The guard couldn't stop his distressed protest.

"Your Royal Highness." Pierre bowed to Kat. "Do you love your country?"

"Of course."

"Then how can you let half a million people lose their identity, their history, their cultural heritage, and become lost amongst a sea of a million strangers, when you can stop it. The people need a leader to guide them. They need you."

"It is over, Pierre. She has made her wishes clear," the king said. "Without Stefan, I have no heir."

Kat gripped Logan's hand. Her fingernails dug into his palm.

He met her gaze and nodded his understanding.

"Yes, you do, Father," Kat said. "You have me."

LOGAN SAT ACROSS FROM Daniel's hospital bed. "I'm sorry we didn't find out you were alive earlier." Logan fingered his Stetson, and met his friend's gaze. "I should have believed in you more."

Daniel lay back on the pillows, struggling as he took

a breath with his broken ribs. "The duke made it look good. If I'd seen the evidence about the M.O. on the bomb blast, I'd have believed I was guilty, too."

"That doesn't excuse me for not looking into the accusations harder. Connecting all the pieces earlier."

"Sarbonne was a madman—and a sadist. He believed it was his divine right to rule Bellevaux, and the murder and torture he used to try to secure the throne brought him immense pleasure. We may never know exactly how he orchestrated Prince Maximillian's death, but if Stefan's treatment at the duke's hands is any indication, Max suffered a lot before he died."

"But both you and Stefan survived," Logan pointed out. "The duke didn't win in the end."

Daniel's knuckles whitened as dark memories obviously hit. "You don't know what Stefan went through, Logan. I don't know how he took it."

"I suspect I could say the same about you, my friend."

Daniel looked away, and Logan could see his friend's emotions closing off. Daniel's scars would take a long time to heal. Inside and out.

"It's weird the guy who blew up the ranch helped bring down the duke and Victor."

"He'll have to pay," Logan said, "though Kat seems to think since he saved Hayden he deserves leniency. I'm not so sure. The jury will have to decide."

"Your princess is something," Daniel said, changing the subject. "Even terrified, she wouldn't give up. When she pulled out that knife to save her brother and her son…let's just say she's got a spine of steel when it counts."

"Yeah. She's got courage." Logan's heart twisted in his chest, his despair so thick he could taste it.

"You love her."

"With everything in me," Logan said softly. "We could have made it, Daniel. But Bellevaux needs her, and there's no one else to step in as heir now. I have to let her go."

"Logan, she loves you," Daniel insisted. "Don't walk away so easily."

"Easily?" he said in frustration, getting up to pace the room. "There's nothing easy about leaving her and my children! But a queen needs the right man by her side. Not an ex-CIA rancher from Texas, who may still have enemies like Victor Karofsky coming after him."

"Don't you think she should be the judge of that?"

"I can't make this any harder on her than it already is."

"Then take over as captain of the guards. Sergei is dead. Who better to protect Kat than the man who loves her most?"

Logan frowned. "So, I can be her bodyguard, watching from a distance, until the man she needs to marry comes along?" He slapped his Stetson on his knee and moved toward the exit. "I can't do it. I'll come see the kids, but she's made her decision and I'll do whatever I must to support her. Even if that's leaving." He gave his friend one last look. "It's over, Daniel. This is one Cinderella story that ends without a happily ever after."

His footsteps heavy, Logan closed the door quietly and let his friend rest. He made his way to the refurbished throne room. The last time he'd been here an explosion had destroyed so many lives. He'd thought life was painful then. Now, he had to say goodbye to the woman who would always hold his heart.

The king stood at a window staring out at the countryside. Kat stood near him, a vision. The sapphire-blue dress she wore hugged her figure. Her hair was swept up and a tiara rested on her head. She was a true princess. Regal. Beautiful. Out of reach.

Hayden clung to her side. Their son hadn't left Kat since they left the prison. Logan didn't know how long it would take for his little boy's laugh to come back, but Lanie and Gretchen would be here soon. Rafe had hired a jet. They were all set to arrive this afternoon.

Logan longed to take Kat and Hayden into his arms, but with King Leopold's reign shattered, his legacy tarnished, Bellevaux needed Queen Katherine to keep it intact.

What Logan wanted couldn't matter. He moved closer to them.

"What if I'm not the right person?" Kat said to her father.

"You are the only one who can give them hope." The king sighed. "Once I reveal what I have done, they need someone they can believe in, Katherine. That person is you."

Kat tugged at the elegant gown a lady in waiting had provided. She lifted her skirt, revealing a sexy leg and three-inch high heels. "I'm going to break my leg in these shoes."

"A monarch makes sacrifices." The king kissed her cheek. "But there are six pair of your American Roper boots arriving tomorrow. Your other ones lacked a certain…luster."

"You didn't get rid of them?"

"No. I've learned not to discard the good things in my life." He met her gaze. "I was wrong when I didn't contact you for so long. Then, faced with the total loss of my country, and thinking I knew better, I ruthlessly took the safe life you'd created in Texas from you."

The apology stunned Kat. "I don't know what to say."

"Say nothing. Just please, accept my apology. If I've learned anything in the past few weeks, it's that a royal bloodline means nothing without courage and integrity behind it. You, my dear Katherine, have a pure heart, and the strength to fight for what's right and for those you love. Lastly, you have the will of a warrior. Without your bravery, Sarbonne might have won and we all would have perished. Thank you, daughter. Your mother was a good woman, but very stubborn. I did love her, though. She would be proud of you today."

Tears filled Kat's eyes. Had her father given up the woman he loved for the people of Bellevaux, too? If a broken heart was a requirement to rule this country, she had that part covered.

The king stood just inside the balcony waiting for the clock to chime, signaling it was time to address the joyous crowd of loyal subjects outside. Subjects who only knew their kingdom had grown prosperous, but not at what horrific cost.

Kat peered across the sea of smiling faces below. "What if I can't do it?"

Logan came up behind her, his heart breaking. He turned her into his arms. "You have a good heart. You're smart. You can learn. Your father will help you."

She gazed up at Logan. "What about you? Will you help me? I need you with me."

"As your bodyguard?"

"No." Kat swallowed deeply. "As my prince."

He froze in disbelief. "I'm a Texas rancher, not a prince."

"And I'm a Texas cowgirl, not a princess. We'll learn to rule together."

"You need a real prince—another member of royalty."

"No, she doesn't." The king came to them. "Once I

abdicate, she'll no longer be a princess. She'll be the queen. As Queen of Bellevaux, she can marry whomever she wants."

A ruckus at the door drew their attention. Royal courtiers came in bearing documents and the royal seal of Bellevaux. The king laid the documents out on a table near Kat. "Sign these papers, and you and your children legally become my heirs. You will lead my people."

Kat looked over at Logan, the man she wanted more than anything.

Logan cupped her cheek. "You will be an amazing queen."

She took a deep breath. "Will you stay?"

He stilled. "What if I endanger you?"

She laughed. "I'm more likely to endanger you now, Logan. And what could be better than having my own security expert as my husband?"

"You really mean this?"

She grew serious. "I love you. I can't imagine my life without you. You're the father of my children, and you hold my heart in your hands. I can't do this without you."

"I love you, too, and you and the children are all I need." He looked around at the palace that had been so recently filled with horror and now rang with the sound of his still-subdued son's laughter. Soon, his daughter would join them. "This will be strange. I've never imagined living anywhere but the Triple C."

"I know, but we can vacation there. After we rebuild. Our children will spend time on the ranch at least once a year. I don't want spoiled brats running around this palace."

"Me, either."

She smiled at him. "Do you think there are enough

bodyguards in this entire palace to keep Hayden from starting an international incident?"

Logan smiled. "I think our little Houdini may require his own special corps of security guards. The nanny corps. Poor guys won't know what hit them."

She laughed. "I love you, Logan Carmichael."

"I love you, too, Katherine Nelson. Will you be my 'sometimes' Texas rancher wife?"

"Yes."

He held out a pen.

Kat signed the papers.

"Well, then, Your Majesty. You have yourself a Prince Consort of Bellevaux the rest of the year."

Logan pulled her close and kissed her.

"This is overwhelming," she admitted. "I don't want it to change me too much."

"Don't worry. If you start believing your own queenly press, I'll bring you back to earth and have you mucking out the royal stalls—or talking down wild horses." He kissed her nose. "Come to think of it, your horse-whispering skills are going to come in mighty handy during political negotiations."

"Thanks for scaring me to death. Is it too late to run?" she asked with a smile.

"Yes," he said in all seriousness, "because you don't really want to. Your people need you and you were born for this."

He watched the transformation come over her. The final shift from Texas cowgirl to the queen she was about to become.

"I love you," she said simply. "I was born for that, too, and I will never, ever leave you."

The king cleared his throat and stepped onto the balcony. Cheers went up.

"My people, today I have surprising and wonderful news. I have found my long-lost daughter and she has agreed to be my heir and the next Queen of Bellevaux! Our beloved country shall not be annexed, and I now relinquish my throne. Queen Katherine will guide you with wisdom and courage far beyond her years. I bid you welcome her."

Leopold gestured to the doorway behind him. "Your queen."

Yells of approval roared into the room.

"Your country awaits, Your Majesty," her father said with a bittersweet smile.

Kat trembled slightly, but Logan laced her fingers with his and kissed her tenderly.

"Ready, Kat?"

She met his gaze with love and wonderment. "With you by my side, Logan, I'm ready for anything."

"Then let's do this."

Together, with joined hearts and hands, the new Queen and Prince Consort of Bellevaux stepped onto the balcony—and into their future.

Epilogue

The Christmas tree was perfect.

Fabergé ornaments, diamond-studded Christmas balls, fourteen-karat-gold tinsel and Waterford crystal sparkled against the forty-foot-tall pine. Gold-plated walls and a fresco on the ceiling were everything a castle should be.

It still wasn't home.

Kat sighed and tugged at the designer gown that cost more than she'd made in a year before becoming queen. She couldn't stop touching the diamond necklace. Her grandmother's diamond necklace.

It had been in the family for three hundred years.

How had this happened? How had she ended up here? Her new reality made her head ache as much as the tiara.

Logan pulled her back against him and she sagged into his arms. The one part of her new life that she would never, ever doubt.

"All those diamonds making you nervous?" Logan whispered, kissing her shoulder.

She turned in his arms. "How did you know?"

"I know you, my queen." Logan rubbed her temple and she nearly purred as he eased away her tension.

"Mommy!" Lanie cried out.

Her daughter tugged at her dress. "Grandpa's here."

Kat looked across the room. Her father hovered awkwardly in the doorway. The transition had been hard for him, but they were both finding their way in a very strange relationship.

Kat smiled. "Will you join us?"

Leopold's face creased with a smile. "Thank you."

He walked across the marble floor and Hayden ran toward him, his arms opened wide. Leopold picked up his grandson and pushed the blond hair from his face. Her father swallowed. "He has Stefan's look."

Kat studied the portraits along the wall. The king and his family. A family that no longer existed. Her father's eyes turned sad, and she knew he was thinking of Stefan…no, Léon now. They didn't know where he was, they only knew he was alive and healing.

"Don't cry, Grandpa." Hayden clasped Leopold's face in his hands.

"I'm not, my boy. Because you are safe."

Lanie tugged at Leopold's pants. "Santa's coming tonight."

"That he is, little one."

Lanie bit her lip. "Do you think he'll be able to find us in this big house?"

"I would imagine he will. He is magic," Leopold said and settled on the Aubusson carpet near the tree.

Logan bent his head and encircled her waist with his arms, pressing her back against him. "That's something I never would've thought I'd see, Queen Katherine."

She turned in his arms. "Well, Prince Logan, you gave me a fairy tale. We have to live happily ever after."

"Wait, wait," Lanie cried out.

She snagged her little pink purse. The one she'd discovered in the very large crown jewelry collection. She'd batted her eyes at Logan and he'd given in, letting her carry the pink diamond clutch. Tonight only. Lanie smiled, opened it up and pulled out the old silver horseshoe.

"Daddy. Put it on the tree."

"Lanie? How did you…"

She bowed her head. "I took it off our old tree before I went to bed. I likes it."

Logan swallowed at the antique ornament, the only physical remnant of his past life, besides the land. "I don't know, Lanie. This is a pretty old ornament. Look how sparkly your tree is with all its new shiny decorations."

Lanie pouted. "We *have* to put this on the tree. It's special."

Logan knelt down in front of her and hugged her close. "You are a special little princess."

He lifted her into his arms and walked over to the Christmas tree. "Where should we put it?"

Lanie reached out and hung the two-century-old pewter horseshoe next to a priceless Fabergé creation.

Tears stung Kat's eyes as she stared at what remained of Logan's legacy. His family's ranch was gone. His mother's death was ruled an accident and she now rested next to Logan's beloved grandmother.

"It's finished," Lanie said. "Santa will know where we are."

"How do you figure that, my little princess?" Logan asked.

"'Cause the horseshoe is a piece of home," she said simply and squirmed down to play with her brother.

Logan hugged Kat to him. He removed the tiara from her head and held her close. "We have a brilliant daughter," he said softly. "Forget everything around us. This is home. You. Me. The kids. This is all we need. All we'll ever need."

* * * * *

COMING NEXT MONTH from Harlequin® Intrigue®
AVAILABLE OCTOBER 30, 2012

#1383 BIG SHOT
Big "D" Dads
Joanna Wayne

A woman he can't forget... A love she can't remember... And a killer who plans to make sure she never does.

#1384 MONTANA MIDWIFE
Cassie Miles

Midwife Tab Willows delivers more than babies—she vows to deliver justice to a Montana serial killer, with the help of rancher Aiden Gabriel.

#1385 UNDERCOVER MEMORIES
The Legacy
Alice Sharpe

Bodyguard John Cinca has no memory of his past and is running from his future. Can Paige Graham save him from a legacy he knew nothing about?

#1386 THE VANISHING
Mystere Parish
Jana DeLeon

The disappearing village of Cache has been a legend in the Mystere Parish swamps for decades. But Colette Guidry is sure once she and detective Max Duhon find it, they'll also find her missing friend.

#1387 SWITCHED
HelenKay Dimon

When an office assistant gets mistaken for someone else, she has to depend on Aaron McBain, her new boyfriend with plenty of secrets.

#1388 RUNNING FOR HER LIFE
Beverly Long

Tara Thompson suspects that her abusive ex-fiancé has found her. Should she run again or risk both her life and her heart by trusting interim police chief Jake Vernelli?

You can find more information on upcoming Harlequin®
titles, free excerpts and more at www.Harlequin.com.

HICNM1012

REQUEST YOUR FREE BOOKS!
2 FREE NOVELS PLUS 2 FREE GIFTS!

♦ Harlequin®

INTRIGUE®

BREATHTAKING ROMANTIC SUSPENSE

*Something's going on in Conard County's high school…
and Cassie Greaves has just landed in the middle of it.*

Take a sneak peek at RANCHER'S DEADLY RISK
by New York Times *bestselling author Rachel Lee, coming
in November 2012 from Harlequin® Romantic Suspense.*

"There comes a point, Cassie, when you've got to realize
that stuff you got away with as a child is no longer acceptable
or even legal."

Linc paused, realizing he must seem to be going around
in circles. Well, he probably was, between her damned
scent and his own uncertainty about what was happening.

"I'll be honest with you," he said slowly. "I'm wondering
what's been bubbling beneath the surface at the school that
I'm not aware of. That makes me uneasy. On the one hand,
I'm trying to paint it in the best light because I know these
kids. Or thought I did. I don't want to think the worst of any
of them. On the other hand, I guess I shouldn't make too
light of it. There have been three transgressions we know
about with you. Four, if we add James. I'm not going to
dismiss it, but I'm not going to be Chicken Little yet, either.
The mind of a teenage male is impenetrable."

She surprised him by losing her haunted look and
actually laughing. "You're right, it is. And girls aren't much
better at that age."

Girls weren't much better at any age, he thought a little
while later as he drove her home. He'd certainly never
figured them out.

"Thanks for a wonderful time," she said as he walked her
to her door. "I really enjoyed it."

"So did I," he answered more truthfully than he would
have liked. He had to bite his tongue to keep from suggesting

they do it again.

She was still smiling as she said good-night and closed the door.

He walked back to his truck, keys jingling in his hand, and thought about it all, from the bullying to the rat to the evening just past. The thoughts were still rumbling around when he got home.

Something wasn't right. Something. He'd grown up here, gone to school here, been away only during his college years, and now had been teaching for a decade.

His nose was telling him something was wrong. Very wrong. The question was what. And who.

Find out more in RANCHER'S DEADLY RISK
by Rachel Lee, available November 2012
from Harlequin® Romantic Suspense.